The Staff
and the Shield

Book II in the Master Mage of Rome Series

by

D. W. FRAUENFELDER

BREAKFAST WITH PANDORA BOOKS

In association with

True North Writers & Publishers Co-operative

Durham, North Carolina

GALLEY PROOF - NOT FOR SALE

Copyright © 2015 David Frauenfelder

ISBN: 0-99966933-0-0

ISBN-13: 978-0-9966933-0-1

::Salvete - Greetings::

HAEC EST FABULA VERA AUT SIMILLIMA VERI

Based on a true story

CONTENTS

Acknowledgments

Glossary and Notes - The Ancient Wisdom
of Numa Pompilius

Discussion Questions

Author's Note

::I::

"*Fulmen lapidem scindens*," Lucius Junius Brutus yelled to the angry heavens. *Lightning splitting the stone.*

It was raining-- raining as it had most of the winter, except for one thing: this time the fire of Jupiter was arcing across the sky.

Lucius slung a grammarstone into the black night. Raindrops mixed with hail stung his forehead and ears. The stone disappeared into the darkness.

Then a flash, a boom, and an explosion that knocked Lucius flat.

For a sliver of a moment, bright white light flooded the whole hillside: the stone quarry where Lucius practiced grammar; the thick grove of trees that grew all about it; the steps leading down to the caves of Egeria and the *casula*, the hut of Logophilus, his Greek assistant.

Lucius' little world for the past nine months.

"By Jupiter," he whispered, his ears ringing, his nostrils flaring at the telltale sour, burnt scent of an exploded grammarstone. He'd smelled it many a time, fighting against the Etruscan *haruspices*, seers with powerful mirrors who were trying to destroy the shrine of Numa Pompilius.

The explosion hadn't come from thunder. It was the lightning splitting the stone that knocked him over. His grammar had worked.

"By Jupiter, I did it!" he cried, and let out a whoop of joy.

He pulled himself up to a kneeling position—his leggings, like his cloak, were now soaked through from falling into a puddle—but he hardly felt the cold. The storm was moving on, the lightning moving away. Should he try another grammar?

"Stop!" came a thin cry in the distance.

Lucius recognized it as Logo's. They had retired for the night, Logo to his *casula*, Lucius to the chamber in Egeria's caves where his master Glyph had spent so many days and nights mastering the hidden power of the Latin language.

"Stop!" came the cry again, and Lucius turned to see, in the flash of a distant lightning bolt, the spindly, long-limbed figure of Logo hustling up the stone steps with his arms in the air.

"No more explosions!" Logo waved his arms. "You've smashed the bean pot!"

Lucius shook his head and smiled. They met and linked arms, and Logo stood there and caught his breath for a moment. It was just like Logo to be worried about the vessel in which they cooked their porridge and bean stew than for Lucius' safety. For years before Lucius came, Glyph had experimented with the ancient inflections that, he had said, could accomplish anything. Big bangs did not go unheard.

"But didn't you see?" said Lucius. "I named—"

"I did see, and I heard," said Logo. "And now our dinner is on the ground, and Kaneesh has made short work of it."

"Logo, let the dog eat!" Lucius spread his palms to the sky. "I'm telling you I named a lightning bolt. Is that not a wonder?"

"Certainly it is a wonder, and it will stand you in good stead, if ever you are battling a prodigy during a thunderstorm." Logo looked up. A hailstone bounced off his face. "Let's go. This is the kind of weather where you can catch a spirit of chill and your spirit and it will finally go hand in hand to the land of our ancestors."

They picked their way in the dark down the stairs, slippery with all the hail that had fallen. Now and then a flash lit the horizon to the east. The storm was fleeing quickly to the mountains, but the memory of the successful grammar would be with Lucius forever.

"I can do it, Logo," said Lucius. "I can make the heavens obey me."

Logo said nothing. His head was down as he scanned the path in front of him. His sandals slapped in the wet, and he clutched at his cloak as it unfurled in the still-mischievous wind.

"Logo?"

"To the *casula*," was all he said.

When they arrived at the thatched-roof hut, the moon had broken through ragged clouds. In its light, Lucius saw the broken pot. There were no beans left in it, the food that had been meant for the next night's meal. Kaneesh, the lean yellow-furred dog with alert ears and eyes, was sitting on the stone threshold, licking her lips.

"You had a meal, did you, girl?" Logo said, and brushed his hand over her head. She let out a little whine, and slipped into the *casula* when Logo unpinned the heavy tapestry that kept out the winter wind. Once in, she curled up on Logo's bed and was soon asleep.

Logo lit an oil lamp as they hung up their wet cloaks, and he gave Lucius a blanket to wrap himself in. "It will be light soon," he said. "And maybe a little warmer today."

Lucius shivered, as much with cold as with curiosity. What was Logo thinking?

"I think you have done enough," Logo said as they sat down.

"Enough? What do you mean? I'm sorry. I won't do it again, if you don't want." He thought he'd done well. Through the wet winter, he'd studied the grammar that Glyph had taught him. Many a night he had used all the oil in his lamp. He knew the kinds and possibilities, the various word-endings, and purposes for them, that could do marvels when twinned with the power of the grammarstones. Why did Logo think he should stop?

"I'm not talking about the lightning."

"Well, if you think I should--"

Logo put up his hand. "It is time."

Lucius' words froze on his tongue. Logo stared at Lucius, and Lucius could not keep his eyes on him. His eyes rested on the light, then back at Logo. No sound came, except for Kaneesh's warm breathing, and the whistle of the wind that was the stepchild of the passed storm.

"Glyph left orders," Logo said, his voice clear and quiet, "that once you were strong enough, you would need to go on the journey."

"The journey?"

"Ever since we lost the power of the staff—the *baculum*—ever since the Etruscan seers, the *haruspices*, filled it with gold and locked the power of the grammarstones inside it, I knew you would have to go on the journey to find its twin."

"There is another *baculum*? You told me there wasn't." Lucius had thought often, with frustration, at the memory of his foolish loss of the staff. He had spent many hours practicing with the horn shaft with its hinged knob that opened and let a skilled mage fly a grammarstone at its target. In the end he had gotten it back, but the gold remained in its hollow middle, trapping the magic stones inside. Lucius had gotten better with a sling, but it wasn't nearly as good. With a working *baculum*, he could've perfected ten lightning grammars that winter.

Logo put his hand on Lucius' shoulder. "I know, and I hope you will forgive me for it. But you were not ready before. Now you are."

Lucius nodded without agreeing. Maybe he was ready, maybe he wasn't. But for what?

"There have always been two *bacula*," said Logo, hefting an invisible staff in each hand. "Just as there were two sons of Rhea Silvia, Romulus and Remus, who founded the city of Rome two centuries ago. Egeria, the goddess who watches over this place, always intended for Romulus and Remus to have the *bacula*, and to use them to make the city great. But Romulus killed his brother in a fit of rage, and Egeria did not give him a staff, but waited, many years later, until the lawgiver, King Numa, showed himself worthy of one."

"And where did she keep the other one?"

"The traditions of Numa tell us that she held it until the Etruscans came to Rome. When King Tarquinius Priscus, the grandfather of the present king, made himself master of the city, Egeria greeted the Etruscan goddess of the dead, Vanth. They spoke together about the destiny of each other's lands, and when Vanth realized that Rome would be greater, she contrived a plot and stole the stick. She took it back to her home, and there it is still."

Lucius could hardly believe his ears. "An Etruscan goddess has it?"

"That is what the traditions say. We do not know the full story. But if what we have heard is true, the second *baculum* lies in the bottommost cavern of the Etruscan Land of the Dead, guarded by Vanth. And Glyph said, Egeria has always meant for that *baculum* to be in Roman hands, but she has not the power to get it back."

"And I do?" Lucius looked down at his hands, balled into fists. He opened one, and there was a grammarstone he'd held all that time. Strange to think that such a common stone in such a common hand could--

Logo finished his thought. "You said yourself, 'The heavens obey me.'"

"But a *goddess*." Lucius had heard stories of heroes challenging divinities, but he never thought he could do it.

Logo seemed unphased. "We will need this *baculum*, if you are to defeat the Etruscans once and for all. They are gathering their power, and you know they want to destroy this shrine-- burn the scrolls that contain the ancient knowledge of Numa and Egeria. If they can, they will erase Rome from the tablets of the Fates."

Logo was right about the Etruscans, the *haruspices* with their magic mirrors that could banish a person to another world, an eternal prison. They wanted Rome to be Etruscan forever, and would do whatever it took to keep it so. All the centuries of knowledge, the power, Rome's destiny, would be lost if they allowed the Etruscans to have their wishes.

But a goddess!

"When dry weather comes again," said Logo, "they will look for-- and find-- this place, hidden though it is. You know they will. With a *baculum*, you can defeat them." He let the thought sink in for a moment before adding, "And in any case, if Vanth keeps the staff, she-- or someone else-- must use it against us."

Logo was right that they needed the *baculum*. Maybe it wasn't that difficult. Maybe Logo was just making it out to be so. "Is the Etruscan Land of the Dead a spirit world, where only the shades of things can be found?"

"No, not strictly. The Etruscan Land of the Dead is found underground, through a passage in a tomb to the ancestors of Tarquin. There are portals from it to spirit worlds, but the place itself is as real as the Caves of Egeria. That is why the *baculum* you seek is not a shade, like the ones you encountered in the mirror world last year."

Lucius' eyes fell on the spots of black above Kaneesh's eyes. But instead of fur, he saw a dark cavern. Well, he'd been in dark caverns before. He knew what to do.

"Make no mistake: every part of the Etruscan Land of the Dead is guarded. Sometimes it is guarded by physical obstacles, sometimes by spirits. Sometimes by a mirror.

Everything must be defeated. And then, when you get to the *baculum* itself, it is in a chest called in Greek a *thesaurus*, which has no lid and lock. And, presumably, you will have Vanth to deal with as well."

Lucius thought of his sling. How easy would it be to use it in a cavern? Would Vanth even let him?

"You are right to hesitate. It is extremely dangerous. Not even Glyph wanted to try it."

Lucius laughed. "He didn't have to—he had a working *baculum*, and didn't need a second one!"

"True enough," Logo conceded. "And without a working *baculum*, it will be hard to perfect the kind of grammar you need to overcome all the obstacles in front of you. It is a hard thing, but you have learned much over the winter. And…" he lifted his palms. "There is no other way."

"No other way?"

"No. Unless there is another Master Mage of Rome."

Then there was quiet again, and Kaneesh's breathing, and the wind, as Lucius considered. But only for a moment.

"Then I'll do it," Lucius said, slapping his knee. "I'll do it, and maybe I will summon lightning in a cavern. But first, we must fetch--"

All this time, it had been getting lighter outside as the dawn swelled over the wooded hilltops in the east. Now Kaneesh, who had woken under Lucius' stare, stood up. She turned in a circle, slipped down from the bed, and nosed at the opening of the tapestry.

"What is it?" Lucius said.

"A visitor, no doubt," said Logo.

Logo was right. When he undid the tapestry, Kaneesh

bounded off down the path leading toward Lucius' vegetable garden and the outside world. In the distance, through the sparse winter foliage, the light from a torch bobbed up and down, as the torch holder made his way down the steep grade from the ridge.

Kaneesh barked, and there was a voice, a familiar one: Gnaeus, their companion from the town of Portentia, the man who provisioned them with grain, wine, and oil, and who had saved Lucius from the wicked *magus magister* some months before.

"Master," came Gnaeus' voice. "Thank the gods you are all right. We heard the boom. I came as quickly as I could! I have news!"

Lucius said, "Is there trouble? A prodigy?"

Gnaeus arrived, a halo of light around him from the torch. He was a squat young man, with an open, generous face and big round eyes. His eyes were even rounder now.

"Worse!" said Gnaeus. "Master, terrible news!" He wiped his brow. He had clearly been running, and was sweating even in the winter cold.

"Well? Open the wall of your teeth and speak, young man!" said Logo.

"It's Demetria," said Gnaeus. "She's getting married."

::II::

"Demetria, daughter of Istocles and Eodice, is promised in marriage to Nauarchus, son of Antimachus and Laocleia of Massalia."

It was spring in Rome. Up in the hills where Lucius lived, frost and mist lingered, but the city, which was nearer the sea, never got as cold. Wildflowers had bloomed, the winter rains were abating, and everywhere the land was deep green. Grain was tall; the stalks that had been almost drowned in rainwater were now waving in the fresh, warming breeze. The Tiber River was full and sluggish, carrying silt and branches down to its mouth at Ostia.

In all her fourteen years on the earth watched over by the gods, Demetria, daughter of Istocles and Eodice, had always welcomed the greening of the year. Not so this one. Not after her father had promised her to someone other than Lucius Junius Brutus.

"So we announced it," said Istocles, still wearing the toga of a Roman from his appearance in the basilica, the law court, where the king's servants heard of the Greek merchant's plan. All betrothals for the coming June were announced here on the day after the Ides of February and the sixteenth day before the Kalends of March, the favorable date for such things.

The family sat around the central hearth of their home, a fire glowing in it, and hot food in pots arranged around it., steaming and bubbling. This was the betrothal celebration, and Demetria was dressed in a *palla* and *stola*, the garb of a married woman of Rome.

"It will soon be the favorable month for marriage," Eodice told Demetria. "The month of Hera in Rome, June it is called after Juno, the Roman lady of marriage. And you will marry Nauarchus, a fine man and a rich one."

Demetria nodded. *Now-ark-us.* She rolled the syllables over in her head, like grammarstones in her hand. It seemed impossible. Only a few months before, she had been fighting monsters with Lucius and those grammarstones and now-- marriage! It seemed impossible.

When she was first given the betrothal news, Demetria nearly lost her temper. But then she realized that doing so would've meant even more certainly she'd be married to this fine, rich, Nauarchus, whoever he was.

If Demetria had been less headstrong, Father may have waited a year or two more to find a husband for her. Most Roman girls married somewhere around sixteen, for life was short and children were needed. Men waited much longer, until they inherited property from their father. Demetria had been too shocked to ask how old Nauarchus was. Certainly older than Lucius.

Lucius, the reason she ran off to the shrine of Numa last

summer. Lucius, with whom she had shared so many childhood days.

When she returned, there were many tears and scoldings and tight embraces, and her beloved aunt Phane and all the sisters and cousins had wanted to know the whole story. But Father stayed mostly silent through it all, until he had already arranged the match.

"You are an untamable girl," he said to her, "and because of that, you need to become a woman."

By all the gods, it was true. Demetria knew that, despite everything. And this night, after Father asked the goddess Hestia, Vesta in Rome, to bless their food and fire, and keep their family safe, she saw in his eyes his desire to do what was right, what was Greek, though he could not understand the bond between her and Lucius.

"Antimachus is a merchant in the Greek colony of Massalia and his son will one day inherit the family business," said Father. "The family are successful and they have a great house and many slaves. This is a fine match for you, Demetria."

Once she had successfully bottled up her anger, Demetria cried private tears. Of course she was Greek and had been raised to become a wife. But to go to a distant city-- where was Massalia, anyhow?-- and live for the rest of her life with a strange family, that was too much.

Phane had told Demetria the story of Persephone, who became the queen of the Underworld when she married the god of death, Hades.

"What a sad and beastly thing!" Demetria had said. "To be in the dark and damp forever, with tree roots and dirt for her ceiling." She left it at that, and tried not to imagine what must happen to Persephone in that darkness.

Phane said, "Then you should rejoice when you marry, for you will have a fine house and see the sun every day that it shines. Persephone cannot."

But Persephone was luckier than Demetria. She hadn't had anyone else in mind when she married Hades. Demetria did.

The celebration continued around her. Her mother dished out warm bean stew with sausage, passed around disks of fine wheat flatbread, and speared savory chunks of fried fish from a tureen of hot oil. Winter greens in bacon broth melted in one's mouth. It was a sumptuous meal, and one that Demetria would have greedily enjoyed at any other time. But not tonight. She thought of Lucius, studying the grammar of Numa. What feats could he perform now? She hadn't seen him for months, and had only had a few short messages.

Later, in the women's quarters, Demetria lay awake amidst the varied snoring and sighing of the other girls and women in Istocles' extended family, her belly protesting her decision to eat almost nothing for dinner. Finally, she woke Phane, and they whispered together.

"I am going to run away," Demetria told her. "I can't marry this man. I have more important things to do."

"And what are those?" Phane said. She had lost her husband Aristoxenus in a shipwreck, five years ago, after they had had a daughter, Nausimache, who slept next to her and more deeply than any of the other girls. Phane had vowed never to marry again.

"Lucius--" began Demetria, but her aunt stopped her there.

"Lucius Junius Brutus is a Roman whose mother is from a royal Etruscan family. You will not marry him. How difficult is it for you to remember? You are the daughter of a Greek merchant, my dearest one."

"I didn't say I was going to marry Lucius," Demetria burst out, though they both knew she loved him, and Demetria lived for the adventures they had together. "We have an important task," she began, but stopped there. She had never told Phane about the threat of the Etruscan seers.

Phane sighed. "Which you will not tell me, I think. Just like all those times when you were with him as a little girl, making your scratchings on the bark of the poplar trees that lie next to our River Tiber."

"I would tell you if I could, auntie."

"Are you saying that I would tell someone your very secret plans, my dear?"

"You wouldn't, I know. But someone. You. And it's just not..."

"Someone me what? Are you going to tell someone else?"

Demetria wiped away a tear of frustration. "Why does Father have to be so hard?"

"He is Greek. We are Greek. This is the way. And I have never seen a Greek girl so sad at becoming a rich wife."

"Will it really happen? Or is it only a bad dream, Phane?"

"The last we heard, Nauarchus is making the trip from Massalia as soon as the weather is fine enough to sail. He would've been here today, I think, except for storms. May the Divine Twins keep him safe!" she said, and covered her eyes with her hands, then pulled at her hair. A little hank came out, brittle and graying.

Demetria threw her arms around Phane. "Oh, dear auntie!" she whispered into her ear. "I'm so sorry."

"Aristoxenus!" Phane half-whispered. "He was a good man. I shall have no other. You should not be sad to have a living husband, dearest Demetria."

"I won't be. I promise."

"And you won't run away?"

"Phane, don't make me--"

"Promise me you won't run away-- at least stay to see the man. When you see him, Aphrodite may change your heart."

Demetria held Phane tight, but said nothing.

"My brother is right. You are untamable," Phane said, and laughed through her tears.

::III::

"Gnaeus, why didn't you come sooner?" Lucius cried, balling a fist.

Gnaeus Portentius, wrapped in a dry blanket, sat warming his hands at the fire as the sun peeked from the hills. Steam rose from the wet ground.

Logo pulled a piece of hot flatbread from the cooking disk. "Let him eat," said Logo. "It is not a small thing to come from Portentia in a rainstorm."

"I thank the gods for the food that keeps my eyes seeing the sun," said Gnaeus, and smacked his lips as he drizzled oil on the bread from a little beaker beside the fire. He tore a mouthful with his teeth, and chewed noisily. "You know almost as soon as I, master Lucius. The news of the betrothals always comes to us late."

"Indeed," Logo said, turning over a hot circle of dough delicately at its edges with thumb and forefinger. "Today is the Kalends of March. Half a month since the announcement."

Lucius threw up his hands. "She may already be married!"

"Calm," said Logo. "They would not marry her until June."

He began to mold another bread for his own breakfast.

"But they are Greeks! Who says they do things exactly as we do?"

"No one marries yet," said Gnaeus. "That news would have come, too."

"Eat," said Logo. "You have a long road ahead of you."

They all ate, and though Kaneesh the bean-eater begged, she got nothing. Disgusted, she left hanging in the air a smelly reminder of what her breakfast had been, and nipped off to the vegetable garden to hunt for whatever small animal might be after the succulent leaves Logo had planted.

Gnaeus laughed. "The queen has spoken."

"If Demetria is not yet married, we have a little time," said Lucius. "As I was about to say before Gnaeus arrived, we must bring her here as soon as possible."

"Why, master?" said Logo. "Since you are going to Rome yourself?"

"But are we not going on the journey?" Logo hadn't said that Demetria would come along, but if Lucius was going, he wanted her to go, too. She was clever and resourceful; her thoughts ran on different paths from his, but they always met at the right crossroads. He wouldn't have gotten back the gold-filled *baculum* from the Etruscans if she hadn't helped. He wouldn't have accomplished many things without her.

"Journey?" Gnaeus said, cocking his head and closing one eye. He had already gone on one adventure with Lucius and Demetria, and had made a great reputation in Portentia from telling the story of it. But he had never suggested to anyone he would want to go on another one.

Logo said, "We do not need to summon Demetria. The

journey begins in Rome."

"But I thought we were going to the Land of the Dead," Lucius said.

"Dead?" Gnaeus' round eyes widened farther.

"The Etruscan Land of the Dead," Logo said, in a teacherly voice like Glyph's, "can only be entered through the tomb of the Tarquins in Rome. So much I have already told you."

Lucius screwed up his mouth. "But you didn't tell me it was in Rome."

"It is somewhere in the king's palace, in the tombs that lie underneath it. But exactly where, no one knows. You cannot just walk into it. Though it is possible..." and here Logo thought for a moment. "... That one person could find out easier than another."

"You mean Demetria?"

"You have spoken many times about her knowledge of the people and the city. Her way of speaking-- and sneaking."

Lucius was quick to reply. "Without a doubt! In fact, she may already know."

Logo smiled, and Lucius blushed, half in shame for showing his eagerness, half from anticipation of seeing his friend after the long winter.

"So, either way," said Logo. "Your destination is Rome."

"But it is not my-- where I am going, is it, master Logo?" asked Gnaeus. "I've got several lambs coming this season that need looking after."

"We are more than grateful for your service, Gnaeus," said Logo.

Gnaeus nodded, and pointed the uneaten end of his

flatbread at Lucius. "Well, master Lucius, I do wish you good luck. I think it was Hercules last went to the Land of the Dead, and he did make it back, so maybe you will, too." He pulled the blanket closer around him, and added, "And then, I suppose you can have the Lady Demetria or anyone else you want for a bride." And he took a large bite of bread.

"Well said, young man," said Logo, as Lucius blushed the more. "But there is one thing."

"One thing?" said Gnaeus, his mouth full.

"Stay here, Gnaeus. I think we will have need of you."

Gnaeus stopped chewing, and almost dropped his flatbread.

"Rest," said Logo. "Use my bed. Lucius and I will take counsel with each other."

Gnaeus went into the *casula*, and soon, despite mumbled misgivings about the Land of the Dead, was snoring loudly. The sun strengthened, and soon it was warm, and the sky a deep, cloudless blue. Birds whizzed overhead, and a butterfly made its way from wildflower to wildflower.

Logo said, "I do not think you should simply walk in without some kind of protection against the Etruscans."

"We can take the gold out from the first *baculum*," said Lucius. "I may even be able to do it with grammar."

Logo held up his palm. "Do not try that. It's dangerous to do grammar on the *baculum* itself. I have an idea."

Logo's idea was this: for Lucius to return to Rome, but in a kind of disguise. He would go with the *baculum* still filled with gold, and use it as a walking stick. He would pretend to have been made cripple and dull from his time at the shrine, and Gnaeus would be his helper. The Etruscans would see that the *baculum* and Lucius himself were harmless. Meanwhile, he could gather information about the whereabouts of the Tarquins' tomb.

"But you must be able to fool everyone," said Logo. "Including Demetria. If she does not know-- at least at first-- then no one will know. But it will not be easy. The *haruspices* are great readers of signs, and they recognize a lie faster than anyone."

"I will truly be Brutus," said Lucius, excited at the prospect of fooling the *haruspices*. "I will be what the King named me for choosing to be a priest over a warrior."

"It will be dangerous," said Logo. "You will need grammarstones. And your sling."

"I will take them. But I would rather have a *baculum* with no gold inside."

They agreed that Lucius would practice his act as a limping simpleton for a few days, and Lucius studied the lore to see if there was a grammar to make others see him in the way he wished. He found one grammar that said, *homo bruteus factus, may the person be made a fool,* but he didn't find one that said, *may the mage be made to seem to others as if he is a fool.*

"That is a hard grammar to devise, I think," said Lucius. "If only I could strike all the Etruscans with lightning, how much easier all this would be!"

Logo shook his head wearily. "You are still so young!"

The next several nights, Lucius went to bed thinking about a grammar for making him seem to be a fool, without success. But he did successfully perfect one grammar: *genu magi magistri invalidum-- may the knee of the master mage become weak.* He tapped his knee with a grammarstone in his sling, and fell to the ground, unable to stand on two legs. For a few hours he hobbled around, getting used to the cane, until the grammar wore off.

Later, he tried *genu magi magistri validum, may the knee of the master mage become strong,* and his leg immediately strengthened.

"Only make sure it is strong for the walk to Rome," Logo said.

Lucius looked out toward the coast, and the city where he had grown up. Cooking fires made a smudge of haze on the horizon.

"And may I be strong for all that will take place there," he whispered.

::IV::

Lucius and Gnaeus set out for Rome on a fine, bright blue morning the day before the seventh of March, the Nones.

"A good day for traveling," Gnaeus said. "Dry above, not too much mud below."

Lucius was more than ready; he'd studied all the grammars he'd thought he'd use. New leather buskins were made for him for the trip to Rome. And Gnaeus was given a full picture of what he would need to do-- shepherd a simpleton to his father's house, and stay with him until he had found the entrance to the Etruscan Land of the Dead.

And after that, "Home!" Logo insisted. "Not just for your lambs. While you are in Rome, you must stay at the Junius household, and in view of all. The *haruspices* will doubtless be awaiting their chance to capture you and make you tell them where the Shrine is. You, after all, are among the few who will not become lost while looking for it."

Gnaeus went back to Portentia the night before to tell his family he would be gone and to fetch the buskins, and Lucius truly felt he did not sleep at all.

But they walked fast enough that Gnaeus huffed and puffed to keep up. Now and then he would ask for a rest, and at those times his apprehension would show.

"Show me your simpleton," Gnaeus said. "Fool me as if I were the King of Rome."

Lucius stopped in his tracks, drooped his head, crossed his eyes, and left his mouth slack.

Gnaeus was so pleased, he asked Lucius to do it three more times during three more rests. The fourth time, Lucius said "Enough!" and that was the end of the entertainment.

The buskins served well, and they made good time and arrived at the outlying pastures of Rome an hour before sunset, when Lucius took the *baculum* from where it was tied to his back, perfected the grammar on his knee, and took on the vacant look of one who must have been too long in the caves of the prodigies.

Soon, they met herders driving cattle back for the night from the fields swollen with green grass. They stood and gawked as Gnaeus explained what had happened to the unfortunate Lucius Junius Brutus, and then took the story to the city, where everyone soon knew the sad news. Lucius was limping up to the gate of Rome near the grove of Egeria, where he had begun his journey last summer, when he was met by none other than Marcus Junius Brutus the younger, Lucius' elder brother.

"Welcome home, Brutus!" said Marcus, who was driving a cart pulled by two oxen. "We shall have you well in no time." He hopped down from the cart, embraced Lucius, and then helped him and Gnaeus into the cart. Lucius sat as the wheels turned in mud and then on to the hard stones of the Via, the main street of Rome.

Lucius longed to ask Marcus a thousand questions, but he had to bite his lip and avert his glance from his beloved brother. This was harder, he thought, than fooling the Etruscans. And he didn't know whether he could reveal his secret to anyone. Better for no one to know, Logo had said, including Demetria.

Demetria. She came along with, it seemed, every resident of Rome as Marcus drove the cart toward the Junius family home, near the northeast end of the Capitoline hill. Away to the southwest a stone citadel rose as the last defense of the city, and near there a great temple was under construction. At Gnaeus' bidding, Marcus answered that it was to Jupiter Optimus Maximus, Jupiter Greatest and Best, and that King Tarquin was building many things in Rome, for he wanted to be a good king.

First, however, was Arruns, the son of the king. He was accompanied by lictors, guards carrying bundles of axes bound to a long stick, and the crowd parted as he came. He was not as robust as the boy who had challenged Lucius not even a year ago to swim the Tiber: he was paler, and had not grown.

"Lucius, I greet you in the name of the king," said Arruns, and coughed. "We shall expect you in the house of my father tomorrow."

He took Lucius' hand, but Lucius acted as if he did not know him. Arruns exchanged glances with Marcus, and stood for a moment, his eyes wide with puzzlement.

Then Demetria herself climbed into the cart, greeted Arruns and Marcus, embraced Gnaeus, and took Lucius' hand, who crossed his eyes so that there were two of her. Blood came from his lip now, he was biting it so hard, and he forced himself to focus on the top of her head, which no longer was topped with black, curly locks, but the head scarf and veil of a woman to be married.

"I cannot be here long," she said. "My father-- Lucius--" She looked into his eyes, shook her head, and stifled a cry. "Lucius?"

He said nothing, and she averted her eyes.

"Come, Demetria," called Arruns, who was already standing on the ground. He took her hand as she stepped from the cart. "You know you should not be here."

Demetria looked back before the crowd swallowed her. Lucius stared at her, and it was all he could do not to cry out.

"*Arana Atana*," she cried out as Hesperus helped her down from the cart. It meant *Farewell, Friend*, in the secret language they had created as children long ago.

Atana nanalasa, Lucius whispered. *I will see you soon.*

Marcus clapped him on the back. "What did you say, brother? Do you speak Latin, or Etruscan?"

As the cart could go no further up the hill with the crowd about it, Marcus waited for their father and mother to come, and they climbed up, greeted Lucius, and spoke to the crowd.

"We are grateful to have our son back from the shrine of Numa Pompilius," said Marcus Junius the Elder. "And now, if you will all go home, we also would like to do the same."

Lucius recognized many in the crowd, including a number of boys who had been his friends and colleagues in the boys' council of Rome. Even Arruns, the prince of King Tarquin, had found his way there. He had lost weight since Lucius had seen him last, and his face was thin and pale, as if he had been sick.

Once in the house, the family surrounded him, including Lucius' boyhood nurse, Gallia. She looked him in the eye and began to weep.

This is too much, Lucius thought to himself. *I can lie to Arruns, to the Etruscans. But my family? Logo didn't know it would be this hard not to be myself, to turn away from Marcus and Demetria.*

Everyone in the household embraced Lucius. Just when he could stand the pain in his knee no more, his mother said, "Let him be. Find a chair."

They went from the front room to the *tablinum*, the place where Marcus the Elder received visitors. There was a table here, and a large chair for Father, and stools for visitors. Lucius was made to sit on a stool as everyone examined him and stared at him.

There were questions from everyone, none of which Lucius answered. Father wondered aloud how this had happened, and Gnaeus said that he didn't know, but there were mysteries in the caves of Egeria that must have been most disturbing. For a simple shepherd, he made the deception come off beautifully.

"But I don't understand," said Junia, Lucius' mother. "He is not looking for mysteries in that place. He is to study the knowledge and guard it."

Father said, "We do not know everything about the shrine of Numa. It is a place of the gods."

"May his genius protect him!" Gallia burst out.

Marcus said, "He shall soon be put right. We will help him. Away from the shrine, his mind will return and so will his strength. And then he can be a warrior in the army of King

Tarquin, as I am. He is not such a bad king, I find."

"Perhaps it is my fault," said Mother. "Lucius is Etruscan from my side of the family. Maybe the Etruscans are not meant to go to the shrine. Maybe a Roman god has cursed my son."

Father frowned. "It is not anyone's fault he is like this, except a god or a spirit."

Lucius could bear it no longer. "Want-- to sleep!" He blurted, and rested his head on his hands. "Go to sleep!"

"Of course," said Mother. "He is exhausted after such a long walk. Gallia, take him to his room. The bed has been made. You--" he motioned to another slave-- "bring him some food and see if he will eat something."

They tried to take his traveling cloak and *baculum*, but he held them close. The grammarstones were under the cloak in a small leather pouch strapped to his side.

Gallia helped him into bed and offered him apples and soft cheese. Even though Lucius was hungry, he refused it, thinking that he would need something to take with him on his walk back to the shrine. It would be long and hard-- and dark-- and he would need to find a way to get out of the city after the gates closed, but there was nothing else he could think of to do.

The sun had set, and the last glow of twilight quickly faded from the window of the small bedroom. Lucius' thoughts whirled about him as he lay there in his heavy cloak and with the gold-filled cane next to him. He had slept here a thousand nights, but now nowhere else in the world seemed more alien to him.

Demetria! He would find her. They would go back to the shrine together. He would find a way to have a working *baculum*, he would study the power of making lightning, and at a point he would not need to get information from the Etruscan *haruspices*. He would simply blast them from this world to the next.

With a prayer to his genius on his lips, he retrieved his sling and grammarstone from his bag, ready to touch his knee with the grammar that would restore his strength. *Just a moment to rest*, he thought, *and gather myself. I will need all my wits about me.*

He lay back and his head felt the familiar comfort of his boyhood pillow. And that was the last thing he knew that night.

::V::

The spirit of sleep that had inhabited Lucius Junius Brutus did not leave him until the sun was up and strong the next day. The first he knew of the day came with Gallia's gentle touch of his shoulder.

"You will see the king today," she explained, in the same voice she used to use when he was a small child.

Lucius silently cursed his laziness. If he had not slept so hard, he could be well on his way back to the shrine with Demetria.

But as he came to himself again, he realized something had changed. His genius-- his spirit twin-- had returned to him some of his courage. It was often like this in the morning. Better than last night, he remembered the reason why they had decided to make him Brutus-- the Simpleton-- and concentrate on finding the tomb of the Etruscan kings.

"The king, master Lucius," Gallia was saying, her hand in his. She was a slave from the northern reaches of Italy just over the mountains, a captive of war from an Etruscan campaign.

Her hair, now graying, was blonde originally, her skin paler than most Romans', and her face was narrow and nose straight and slender. She had stayed with him day and night for the first years of his life; she knew him better than he her, for his memories of his youngest days were fuzzy and infrequent. But she was always fiercely loyal, supporting him in every way.

Could he tell her the truth? Could she help him along, bolster his courage? He didn't think she would reveal his ruse, but he couldn't be sure.

Gallia took his face in her hands. He looked away from her, trying with all his might not to say anything. "Oh master Lucius," said Gallia. "Has an ill-omened god visited you? May your genius protect you."

If only I could see Demetria and tell her everything! Lucius thought over and over again. Then they could find the tomb together.

Gallia helped him out of bed and showed him new clothes laid out for him-- a *toga virilis*, the formal wear of business and ceremony for young men.

Standing as Gallia arranged the elaborate folds, Lucius realized that his lame-knee grammar had worn off, and he would not be able to say it with Gallia there. But he was able to lean on the *baculum* and drag his foot a bit enough to know that it would be all right, he could play it for lame.

He ate some flatbread dipped in olive oil and drank some wine mixed with water. He surprised himself by asking for another bread, and his family, grouped about him, smiled to each other. Lucius rejoiced as well in the familiarity of the drink and the stony aftertaste of the well water he had drunk his whole life, so different from the spring water at the shrine of Numa.

Then his father and brother took him in hand for the audience with the king. They helped him down the slope of the Capitoline and along the Via to the Palatine Hill, where Tarquin had his hall, a palace made of wood in the Etruscan manner. The midpoint between, the Forum, was always crowded with men and animals, and as Father was an important man in town, all greeted him, and many stopped them to express their condolences concerning Lucius.

Lucius was relieved when finally they made the summit of the hill, passing the pavement of audience, where not even a year ago Lucius vowed to be a priest of Numa Pompilius.

The palace of the king stood next to the pavement, up several steps, its triangular porch roof held up by two sturdy oak pillars. The door was oak as well, with marble door-posts and lintel.

As they waited for the door to be opened by the janitor, the doorkeeper, Lucius thought of the *dokana*, the door-posts leading from the Mirror-World to the caves of the prodigies. Demetria had been with him then, and Gnaeus, too.

They moved into the atrium, the hall of entrance, where they waited until the king came to greet them. The roof of the atrium was open to the sky, and the sun made a square of light on a patch of wall, illuminating paintings of Etruscan warriors and priests.

With the king came the *haruspica* Turanquil. The side of her face was burned from the fight she'd had with Lucius the prior summer, and her ear was folded over on itself. A bright pink burn scar disfigured her cheek. But her eyes were just as alert as ever, and her stare bored into Lucius. It was difficult to stand there with vacant-seeming eyes, difficult not to blush or otherwise in any way notice that Turanquil was studying him. He leaned on his *baculum* and crossed his eyes as he had done with Demetria the day before.

"It is the staff that has done this to him," said Turanquil immediately after they had spoken their greetings. "Take it from him, and he will be restored."

Lucius hunched over the staff and clutched it to his chest. Turanquil herself was pretending as well-- she had not said anything about taking the staff, or of losing it again. Something about her battle with Lucius must remain a secret form Tarquinius, but Lucius did not have time to think about that now.

"You see?" said Turanquil, pointing as Lucius bent over. "The spirit of the staff wishes the young man to stay in its thrall."

"The staff is an ancient symbol of our people," said Father. "No one will take it from a priest of Numa."

"He is no priest," said Turanquil. "A priest has control of his thoughts, and can speak them. A god or demon has taken this one's wits."

"It is not the staff," said Father. "He has been taught to keep it, and thank the gods for this. We will care for him as best we can. If we cannot make him better, then we will send to the healer Apollo and the oracle at Delphi for an answer. Nothing like this has ever happened to our people before."

Turanquil set her jaw. "It is past time for the Etruscan gods to be made master of this so-called shrine of Numa, and to learn what it is Romans do there. Or else, do you wish, king, for more of your subjects to be changed into this?"

The anger of Turanquil felt to Lucius as hot as the fire from a forge, and yet he shivered from it.

Marcus the younger bristled. "We shall not--"

"By Tin," said the king, using the Etruscan name for Jupiter, "Peace. No more talk of Rome and Etruria. That is for another day. We do not take, but give now. It has been long since the Junius clan reclines at dinner with the Tarquinii."

Lucius sighed. He was already exhausted from keeping up the ruse; maybe a meal would help. But Turanquil's stare made him want to run away as far as he could. *My genius protect me*, he thought. *Only be patient.*

They progressed through the house to a dining room that opened onto a large interior garden. Couches had been set up next to a table filled with hard-boiled eggs, bowls of salt, and vinegar sauces. They lay down on the couches, and the king said a prayer of thanksgiving to the gods for the bounty of the table.

"Is Arruns called away?" asked Father when they had settled themselves. "He is a friend of my son. It would do him good to see him."

"Alas, he is ill!" said Tarquin. "He has worsened since Lucius went to the shrine. A demon of his lungs. He must stay abed often. But later we will visit him, if he feels strong enough."

"And your mother? She has also been ill, I know."

"By Apollo, she has been better the last few days and has taken some broth," said the king, dipping an egg first in sauce, then in salt. "But that has not stopped our artisans from continuing the process of painting her tomb. She has had very specific instructions. And she has wanted to see it finished before she dies. But she is too ill to be moved."

Father said, "Has she chosen a bloody Greek story to entertain her while she lies in her tomb? I know you Etruscans favor that kind of painting."

"Blood nourishes the dead," said the king, and made a sign to ward off the evil eye. "But my mother is also particular about the carving of animals on her tomb. She wants to be guarded by twin lion-sphinxes, an animal we know from the kings of Egypt. And such things must be imbued with the proper spirit."

Turanquil spoke. "It is not an easy thing to create a lion-sphinx who will truly guard a tomb."

"But your people are able," said Father.

"We have lore," said Turanquil.

"I would see these sphinxes when they are ready," said Marcus.

"Part of the defense is that no one knows where they are," Turanquil began, but Tarquinius put his hand up.

"It would please me to show you the tomb," he said. "For it is a wonder already, though unfinished."

"But King--" Turanquil tried.

"Enough," said the king. "We are among family."

Lucius could hardly believe his luck. They finished the meal, and after what seemed to him an eternity of pointless conversation, the king led them down a passageway to a storeroom.

"You bury your dead with the grain?" Father asked.

"Only watch," said Tarquin. He motioned to a row of jars deeply embedded in the floor, each with its own mouth, closed with a painted ceramic lid. All of the lids were as long as a man's forearm. "One, two, three, four." He counted lids, stopped at the fourth, and removed it. Then he reached in and seemed to turn something.

"Stand clear, young Brutus," said Tarquin.

Lucius didn't need to play the fool to stumble out of the way as a portion of the floor opened beneath him, its mechanism hidden in the jar.

"A god thought of this," said Marcus the Younger as he peered into the darkness that seemed to seep from below.

"We shall need lamps," said Father.

"We prefer candles," said the King. "The smoke does not stain the paintings as readily."

With a grammarstone, thought Lucius, *I could light that place like the sun.*

Candles and candleholders were stored on shelves nearby, and each of them got one except Lucius. The flickering of the lights as they walked down stone and wood stairs made shadows leap up onto the walls and then down again, and the sweet smell of the beeswax freshened the musty place.

"Long ago, all Etruscans buried their dead underneath the house," said Tarquin. "This is a very old practice. Nowadays there are those who make stone houses of tombs and set them one next to the other. But we hew to the old ways."

"It is well," said Father. "Thieves cannot steal from a guarded and hidden place."

"And there must be much gold there," said Marcus the Younger.

And other things, thought Lucius.

It was cold and damp below, and the corridor, stone-walled, had seeped water. The workmen had put planks of wood on the floor to step over the puddles. The ceiling, rock smoothed into an arch, was almost tall enough to walk under without stooping.

The king said, "Once the rains leave us, this will be dry and cool, a good place to store grain if need be."

The corridor opened into a chamber with a threshold on its far side and a smooth, straight wall on either side of it. A triangle of wall topped the threshold.

Paintings had been made on each of the smooth spaces next to and above the door. Above the door, lions met, their front paws outstretched. On either side, twin warriors stood, one with a spear, the other with a sword.

"This is the entrance to the tombs of the Tarquinii," intoned the king. "Let no one enter with ill intent."

The king's pronouncement coaxed everyone into silence, and all made a sign to ward off the evil eye as they passed the first threshold.

Once inside, the king spoke in a more relaxed voice. "Outside you saw the divine twins who guard the door between death and life. We have passed through the doorposts into the place where we honor our dead and see them to their journey below."

The room into which they had passed was large, and high-ceilinged-- too tall even for a tall man such as Marcus to reach up and touch the arch of the vault. As they turned about with the lamps, paintings could be seen on all four sides. Two further thresholds went off at right angles as well as one on the far wall. Two more openings could be seen at the right and left corners of the far wall, and each of these had sculptures on either side.

"As you can see, there are doors and doors," said Turanquil, and pointed to the two thresholds to their right and left, on the side walls. Lucius looked carefully at them, and realized that they were only paintings of doors. On one, the door was painted with a dark brown, with thick posts and lintel, and on the door itself there were bright yellow circles, one after the other, both in a band across the door's middle, and along the inside of the post and lintel.

Marcus, gazing on the door, said, "This one must lead to a treasure house! It is the heaviest and strongest door I have ever seen!"

The king nodded. "The door to the Land of the Dead is closed forever from within and without. Only spirits, who are nothing but wind, may enter!"

This door was flanked by two men in Etruscan dress-- long robes, headdresses, and slippers with toes gathered into a point. They were priests whom Lucius recognized as those who did the ceremonies to the dead.

The other wall also had a door, not nearly as armored. On either side of this were scenes of hunting, and birds flying overhead.

"Beautiful," said Father. "Your painters are extremely skilled."

"Greeks taught them well," said the king.

"Again, there is no way through this door except for spirits," said Turanquil. "It is a door of those who die in the wilderness and whose bodies cannot be found."

The far wall had another false door, and this one had scenes of seafaring, along with twin seahorses ridden by gods were painted on each side. Lucius thought this must be the door to the Underworld for those who died at sea, but they passed it by without comment.

To the left, another passage opened, and here was where the lion sphinxes made their appearance. They were hardly more than blocks of stone, but the animals were beginning to emerge, jutting heads crowned, shoulders endowed with wings.

"They have not been consecrated yet," said Turanquil. "But once they are, beware those who attempt to rob."

Lucius wanted to ask what Turanquil and the *haruspices* would do to the sphinxes to make them protect the tomb, but contented himself with admiring the stone, which was flecked with orange and silver and reminded him of the stone in the quarry at the shrine.

They went in, stooping, and found the place in the wall where the king's mother would be laid. On each of the side walls there were unfinished paintings: on one side, what looked like a monster with a vulture's beak and donkey ears; lines of paint curved out from it. On another, a goddess carrying a torch. The third was the most detailed: women carrying water next to a picture of a woman raising a dagger against a sleeping man.

The younger Marcus immediately turned to the third picture. "It is of the Danaids!" he said, wonder tinging his voice. "Those women who murder their husbands in their beds are punished with toil in the afterlife."

"The daughters of Danaus," said the king. "They were from Egypt, and so my mother liked this story to go along with the sphinxes."

"Certainly she did not do this to her husband?" asked Marcus.

"It was disease that killed him. She was widowed very

young, and I never knew him," said Tarquin. Lucius had learned from Arruns, who had tutors to teach him history, that Tarquin's father, a son of Tarquinius Priscus, had died under the kingship of Servius Tullius.

Arruns had also said that his great-grandfather, Priscus, was killed by Romans who did not want the Etruscans for their rulers. At the time, Lucius had wondered why Romans would want to do such a thing. To him, Etruscans were the rulers, and Romans the ruled. There didn't seem to be any reason why anything should change.

But that was before he knew about the lore of Numa Pompilius and the power of the Latin language. He didn't want anything to happen to that, and he didn't want the *haruspices* to destroy it.

"Here, the goddess Vanth," said Tarquin. "Who watches over all the dead. And there, Tuchulcha, her servant."

"The lines here are to be the serpents that coil about him," said the younger Marcus, tracing the brush strokes with a finger. "Is that not so?"

Turanquil nodded. "Tuchulcha is a guardian here and below. When this is finished, few who rob will stay when they see this."

Lucius then had an idea that became something spoken aloud before he even wished it: "See more!" he said. "More pictures. More lions. Goddess."

"The young priest speaks," said Marcus. "Brother, do you like the tombs?"

Lucius nodded vigorously. "Other rooms, other stairs!" he said, and motioned with his free hand, the other clutching the knob of the *baculum*. Was it possible to find the entrance to the

Land of the Dead simply by asking?

"This is the only place of the Tarquinii," said the king. "Some day, by the good grace of our ancestors, we may rule Rome long enough to have a city of dead kings."

Turanquil stared at Lucius, who bowed his head and turned away from her. "He is curious for a simpleton."

"His mind is sound, Lady," said Marcus the younger. "But it is as you say. A curse is laid on it."

"Still, may I ask him a question?" Turanquil leaned forward, toward Lucius.

"You might not receive the answer you seek," said Father.

"Lucius Junius Brutus, what door in this tomb leads to the Land of the Dead?"

Lucius tried not to react. He knew she was hoping he would betray himself. But before he even thought I must not answer, his shoulders hunched and his eyes darted out and around the room.

"He understands," Turanquil said.

All eyes fell on Lucius, who looked up at the ceiling.

Turanquil took a mirror out of the fold of her dress. "If he would look into this, we would see his true self. And any ill intent he may have against Etruria."

Marcus scowled. Father put up his hand and was about to speak. But the king spoke first.

"Away with that, Lady. Your arts are not needed at this time. I said before, we are among family."

"But family is not always true to family," said Turanquil, and motioned to the paintings of the Danaids. "One day, perhaps Romans will destroy Etruscans. Is that what you want?"

Then there was a silence, long and tense, for all knew that Turanquil spoke truly.

"Lady," said King Tarquin finally, and with exaggerated patience, "you dishonor our guests. Put the mirror away. And let us take our leave, for the spirit of cold is entering my bones."

When they re-emerged, Lucius shielded his eyes from the light. The sky outside, though piled with cloud in the west, was deep blue.

"It is good to be alive, is it not, my brother?" Marcus said, and thumped Lucius on the back.

"Sky bright, not painting," Lucius said.

"Brutus, simpleton, you are wise," said Marcus. "The sky is much better than gazing at paintings underground. May you never have to go back there."

Marcus took Lucius by the shoulder and turned him towards home. They walked side by side for a few steps, and Lucius' spirit soared to be with his brother. *I will tell him about this as soon as I can*, he thought. *We will be together in this.*

Lucius turned and saw Turanquil, her ruined ear, her hand in the fold of her dress, speaking to King Tarquinius Superbus, Etruscan ruler of Rome.

"Don't worry about her, brother," Marcus said. "You have fought her well and will do so again, I know. Never fear. You shall safeguard the destiny of Rome. You will save us, priest of Numa."

Lucius looked up at his brother in wonder, wordless. Marcus smiled, and they made their way home.

::VI::

Demetria woke to news: a Greek bireme-- a ship with two banks of oars-- had put in at Ostia the night before, much battered by wind and sea, but with all hands safe. They were carrying a cargo of lavender, a prized herb for scenting perfume, and the navigator was a tall, handsome man who, so the story went, had saved the ship more than once during the voyage.

"The crew will be in Rome before the sun turns in the sky," said Phane.

Demetria ran a hand through her tangled hair. She had neglected to braid it the night before. "Is this he? The one father has chosen?" She didn't know whether to be excited or afraid-- though she was both without even willing it.

"Yes, dearest, it is Nauarchus," Phane said, and embraced her. "They say he knows the sea better than Poseidon! And is as handsome as Apollo the archer."

"What am I to do?" Demetria cried.

"Why, get ready, girl!" Phane said. "Your fiancé cannot come to see his bride and find Artemis, the mistress of wild animals. He must see Aphrodite, the goddess of love!"

It was true. Demetria's mother, Eodice, who had woken early and been at work for hours, came back into the women's quarters and announced they would be having Nauarchus and his crew for a meal in the afternoon, once he had arranged for repairs of the ship and floated upriver to Rome from the harbor.

"You will see him today," said Eodice. "And you had better behave yourself, or you will find yourself the unhappiest girl in Rome."

"Will we be betrothed tonight?" Demetria asked.

"You are already betrothed, daughter," said Eodice. "This is the presentation. And the marriage is set for the month of June. I have sent for women to prepare you. Now." She called for a slave, who brought in a chest. Eodice smiled as she unclasped it and opened it. A smell of new linen, cedar, and lavender wafted from it, thrilling Demetria. Mother pulled a shining white dress from the chest, fine and soft.

"By Hercules," Demetria whispered.

"No, poor Demetria! You should swear by all the Graces," Phane said. "It is a wonder to behold!"

"And it is not even your wedding gown," Mother said, more than a hint of pride in her voice. "I wove this myself, and there is only one flaw in it, and I would dare you to find it, by Athena." She turned it over and over, passing her hand on the fine fabric.

Demetria reached out to it, but Mother pushed her away. "Only the skin of women who have bathed and oiled will touch this dress," she said. "Now, if you wish to wear this, then you will pay attention and sit still while you are readied to welcome your fiancé."

Mother was going to put the dress back in the chest, but Demetria had caught sight of something bright in the bottom of it.

"What is that?" she asked.

"That is your zone," Mother said. She took it out, a long belt of woven linen threaded with gold and silver in a meander pattern. Red gems twinkled amidst the metal. She put her hand to her chest as she spoke of it. "Your father worked very long and hard to afford this. It is from Troezen, in Greece. There is no finer belt to beautify a skinny young girl. See." And she held out the belt to her.

It was so dazzling that a tear fell down Demetria's eye-- against her will. The zone was the one piece of apparel that told a Greek girl that she was a woman. It surrounded not only one's waist but crossed also in the center of the chest, so that the Greek gown Eodice had made, which was long and loose, would hug Demetria's body.

Hercules had fought the Amazon queen Hippolyta for her zone, for it was magic.

Mother saw the tear, and prayed, "Ah, may the jealousy of the gods pass you by, dear Demetria!" She held her hands in the air with the zone in one palm. "There is no daughter more blessed than you. May you live in peace and quiet all your days. Leave off from this childish adventure you have loved so much."

And with that, she replaced the zone and the dress and closed the clasp on the chest. "Phane," Mother said, "I leave you in charge of this poor merchant's princess. I have a full day of seeing to this meal, and as much as I would like to wrestle with your curls, Demetria, I haven't time. We are not having barley porridge, I can tell you."

After Mother left, in came slaves. Some readied a tub and poured hot water into it carried from the kitchen fire. They bathed Demetria, rubbing her all over with oil and then scraping it off, along with dried sweat and dirt, using thin metal rods called strigils. They anointed her with perfumed oil that smelled of spice and tickled her nose. Then they spent a long time combing out her curls, oiling them, and arranging them behind a hair band.

Demetria did not spin wool that day. She spent the entire morning in the women's quarters, trying not to mess up her hair, breathing in the spiced fragrance of the oil. It was agonizing. She could not even play with Phane's daughter, who ran and screamed all about the quarters, and dressed herself in a wedding dress made of her own blanket.

Phane's prediction that the Greek sailors would be in the house before the turning of the sun-- noontime-- did not come true. In fact, the sun was well in the western sky, its rays slanting weaker and weaker through the window in the women's quarters, before finally the slaves came back with makeup.

The slaves whitened Demetria's cheeks and painted her eyes, then put spots of red over the white. They brought in a bronze mirror so she could see the final effect, and as she took the mirror, she prayed aloud to her genius:

"May we stay in separate worlds, o my dear one!"

The slaves laughed, thinking that Demetria didn't

understand the mirror was only showing her reflection, not her genius in another world. They were used to women looking at mirrors. They were not, however, familiar with the magic mirrors used by the Etruscan *haruspices*.

What Demetria saw shocked her-- the bronze did not show a perfect reflection, of course, as one would see in a pond or a puddle when the sun came out after rain. But the Demetria in that oval was a Demetria she had never seen before. One who looked like a woman, not a girl who had run with boys her whole life, sneaking out of the house, climbing trees, hiding in stands of grass to hear conversations she was not supposed to hear.

"I am a silly painted Medusa," Demetria declared.

"You are not!" cried Phane, throwing her arms around Demetria's neck, but careful not to touch her face or hair. "Nauarchus will be enchanted with you. Your beauty is like that of the immortals."

Demetria felt more tears coming, but knew that it would cause a terrible uproar if she smudged her makeup. So she swallowed hard, and said, as much to herself as to Phane, "Well, calm down. By Hercules!"

"You are going to need to stop swearing by him," said Phane. "Swear by Hera, the mistress of marriage."

Suddenly, Eodice burst in. "Get on your clothing, girl," she said. "Nauarchus and his crew have arrived. We must present you. By Hera! Stop dawdling! And don't cry, girl."

"I wasn't," Demetria said, but the slaves had already sprung into action, surrounding her and bringing the dress over her head, carefully letting it down over her so that the fabric would not brush against the makeup. Then the zone, tightened behind her back, and thin bracelets of gold for her wrists.

"You will have more jewelry from the man himself," said Phane. "You must give him the pleasure of giving you much gold."

Finally, she was given a circlet of silver to wear over her temples and forehead. Hanging from the crown was a transparent veil, that left her eyes uncovered but the rest of her face in mystery.

Demetria was in a daze. The smell of the dress, heavy with lavender, mixed with the perfume and made her head spin. Her head felt heavy under the crown and veil.

Then the smell of dinner began to waft in through the open door of the women's quarters. Mother had prepared a very elaborate one, and the smells were rich and heavy. Demetria realized she had not eaten all day-- had hardly had a drink of water, even.

She didn't know what finally got her-- the powerful smell of fish stew and silphium, a stinky herb she had never liked-- or the pork sausages boiled in duck fat, a thick kind of smell that seemed to clog her nose and ears, and settle on her eyelashes, making it hard to see.

But when she finally was led into the main room, with the dishes and pots all arranged around the glowing hearth fire, crocks of salty goat cheese, barley cakes warming, and a dozen or more dark Greek men with black, curly hair and beards sitting on low stools around it, she only had time to see one of the tallest of the men, and certainly the most handsome, stand up, before she began an uncontrollable coughing and sneezing fit.

The most powerful of the sneezes brought her to her knees

and sent the crown with the veil went flying. She tried to cover her mouth, but instead her hands sledded across the layer of white foundation on her cheeks. Slaves who enveloped her with a large napkin further smudged her face.

She heard her father apologizing for her, but could not make out what Nauarchus said in reply.

"Fresh air!" she managed to gasp. "Let me breathe."

She was carried out of the hearth room, and into the courtyard of their house. She leaned on the old olive tree that grew in the center, and all the attendants surrounded her, some asking what they could do for her, others saying to keep away and give her breathing space. Another brought the crown and veil, and tried to put it back on her head, but she knocked it away, and it rolled along the pavement and into a puddle where a brick was missing.

"Water!" Demetria said. "Let me go to the well."

"But we have water here," said an attendant, motioning to a nearby jar.

"The well!" Demetria said again, and fell to her knee, partly to get her point across.

They all helped her up and out of the house. The neighborhood well was a short walk from the house, a place where women congregated with jars to draw water and exchange gossip. The attendants let down a bucket, and brought it up for Demetria. She took a long drink, letting the water splash on her dress. Then she splashed her face, and the water was gray with makeup as it dripped from her.

"Go, tell my mother I am feeling better," she said, and it was true. She did feel better. "All of you. I will stay here until I am fully recovered."

They left, wide-eyed, against their better judgment. But being slaves, they were required to obey.

Demetria watched them go. "At least," she thought to herself, "I will not have to marry this man, for there is no way that he will want me after what he saw." And then she hiked up her skirts and ran.

::VII::

Demetria ran. She ran down stony paths and through tall green grass wet with recent rain. She ran through wheat fields and cow pastures. She ran through a thicket of oaks where pigs rooted for acorns. One pig looked up and snorted at her. "Hello, Smugglemouth," she called, for she knew this one. It was a familiar road for her.

Two more hours remained, perhaps, before sunset. It would be a cold walk to the shrine of Numa Pompilius, but it was the only thing she could see doing. But first, she had to collect Gnaeus and Lucius. It made no sense for Lucius to be a simpleton. If anything, he had become smarter while under the care of Glyph!

In any case, she would rather be with a simple Lucius at the shrine than with a sea captain in Massalia.

The back side of the Capitoline Hill was steep, with few paths, and wooded. She scrambled up a ledge of stone, and then swung up another outcropping, her sandals scrabbling on loose shingle. Halfway up, the knob of a root seemed to appear from nowhere and tore the hem of the dress. Three quarters up, Demetria fought through a cobweb and low-hanging branches, and the twigs and pointed evergreen leaves of a holly almost took the dress off her body. She lost time carefully unsnagging herself from every leaf.

May my zone *be untouched!* she prayed to any god that was listening. The belt was truly a wonder. She hoped to find a way to give it back to her mother at the proper time. Or... when she and Lucius...

Enough thinking! She forced herself to concentrate on the climb, and finally gained the summit of the hill, and the houses of the oldest families in Rome appeared before her. The lowering sun was behind her, and the large trees, Italian pine and holm oak shaded the house's backyards, most of which were not cultivated or even cut back, as many were in Demetria's neighborhood closer to the river. There were chicken coops, and now and then a pig pen or a kitchen garden bordered with a wall of stones, but otherwise it was wild and overgrown.

She picked her way until she found a trail that she and Lucius had blazed themselves. It led to their secret shrine where they had made up their language. The path went directly up to the back door of the Junius family house, where there was a small spring that the family used as a place to ask prayers, and the slaves would now and then draw water from, though it was too small for washing clothes. Wildflowers sprung up here as well as long, luxuriant grass at all times of the year. The shed for relieving oneself as well as the garbage pit were here as well, and made Demetria's nose crinkle every time she passed it.

Before all their adventures began, Demetria was a frequent unannounced visitor to the house. She would walk in through the back door, greet the slaves, and continue up a back staircase to the children's rooms in an addition built by Lucius' father. But on some days, she would use a ladder to get up to Lucius' window, tap on the shutter and await a reply, and then scramble down the ladder and into the woods, to be joined swiftly by Lucius.

This is what she chose to do this time. The ladder was hidden behind raspberry canes and grapevines that grew up the back of the sturdy stone house, and it was this ladder she had used to besiege the Temple of Sethlans when Lucius was seeking to retrieve his *baculum* from the *haruspices*.

She pulled the ladder up out of the groundcover, snagged her dress again on the thorns of the raspberries, unsnagged herself, wrestled the ladder up against the side of the house, and climbed. She tapped on the shutter three times in three quick bursts, for a total of nine taps, and waited. If Lucius were in his right mind and present, the reply would come immediately. If not, she had time to wait and tap again.

But was Lucius in his right mind? He couldn't be. Still, they had adventured much and gone to many worlds when she was with him, and maybe something had happened on one of those adventures.

Demetria tapped again: tap-tap-tap, pause, tap-tap-tap, pause, tap-tap-tap. It was getting cooler by the minute with the sun dipping into the foliage of the highest trees behind her, and her feet were beginning to hurt from standing on the rough top rung of the ladder. Still, it didn't matter. She would wait for Lucius, sure that he would reply soon.

It may have been a quarter of an hour that she waited, tapping every so often, before Demetria heard someone below. There had always been that risk-- a slave of the Junius family coming to bring a bucket of scraps to the garbage pit, or someone else to relieve himself. But this was someone-- or rather two someones-- looking for her.

"Mistress Demetria!"

She looked down. There was the round face of Gnaeus, and the kind one of Gallia. Now and then Gallia had been the one to hear the taps, and, indulgent as she was, would bring Lucius to tap back and let him go. She could never say no to him.

This time, however, both Gnaeus and Gallia wore a look of concern, and there was no Lucius with them.

"Mistress Demetria! Come down from there," Gallia half-mouthed, half-whispered.

Demetria did not move. "Where is Lucius?"

"Come down quickly, before someone sees you!"

Demetria wanted to point out to Gallia that she and Gnaeus had already seen her, but she held her tongue. Gnaeus helped her off the ladder and stowed it at her direction.

"You are a sight!" Gallia said when Demetria joined her. "What a beautiful dress you have ruined! This is terrible."

"But, by the gods, I hope the zone is all right?"

Gallia picked out a leaf that had gotten stuck behind the belt, and turned it on each side. "I cannot believe you would fly through the woods wearing such a beautiful thing."

"I had no choice. There was a man whom Father had chosen to marry me."

"Yes, he is a handsome and good man, I'd say," she said.

Demetria stared at Gallia. "How--?"

"He is at the house now, in the atrium, waiting for you," said Gnaeus.

"But when he saw me, I began to sneeze--"

Gallia took Demetria's hand in hers. "Dearest, it is now your time to be married. You must yield to your father's wishes. We cannot do what we wish every time."

"But Lucius. He and I. It's important. Our work."

"Lucius might make a good husband some day. When he is well, and older. But--"

"I don't want to marry Lu-- what I meant to say is-- I can't explain. He's--"

"Wait," came a voice from the threshold of the back door.

The door swung open, and there was Lucius.

"Master, you had better--" Gnaeus began.

"Just one word, Gnaeus." Lucius looked Demetria in the eye, and was about to speak, but she didn't let her.

"I knew it! I knew you weren't a simpleton!" Demetria cried.

"Shhh!" Lucius hissed. "Do you want everyone to know?"

Now it was Gallia's turn to stare. "My Lucius?" she said, her mouth left open after she said it.

"I can't tell you everything," Lucius said, hands outstretched. "This was Logo's idea. He's--"

But that was all he could say. Gnaeus, who was keeping an eye on the door, suddenly began waving his arms, and it startled Lucius.

Quickly, they found out why Gnaeus had wanted him to stop talking. Lucius' mother Junia came out.

"There you are, Demetria! What a fright you gave us!"

Lucius immediately began to lean on the *baculum* and let his head droop.

"Please come. Nauarchus is waiting for you. It was he who had the idea to come to our house. He's asked to speak to you."

Demetria's heart leaped. Why would this man want to talk to her? Full-grown men never spoke to her except to tell her to stop running so fast or to get out of their fields. And Father rarely had more than a word of admonition. What would he have to say? Especially in front of everyone?

Demetria hesitated, gave Lucius a desperate look, and shook her head. Lucius was bent over his cane, but his eyes rose in his sockets to acknowledge her.

"What a day!" Demetria cried, and stumbled into Lucius trying to get by him into the house. Normally he would have embraced her-- she knew he would have-- to stop her from falling, but this time he himself fell into a sitting position, clutching the *baculum*.

"He is so clumsy now!" Junia said. "Gallia, help him." And she hustled Demetria away.

Junia and Demetria rushed through the slaves' quarters and the kitchen, past the courtyard where rosebushes coiled around olive trees. Then through the main part of the house and into the front-- the atrium, with the middle of its ceiling open to the sky.

Nauarchus stood under that opening, next to a small, dressed stone pool that caught rainwater. Behind him stood three of his crew. In that tentative light, Nauarchus seemed wreathed in mist, but his face was unmistakable. Young, much younger than she had expected, with dark, shining skin and a well-trimmed black beard. His eyes were searching and sensitive, with eyelashes as long as a dairy cow's. Tight black curls framed his face. His jaw was square and mouth set in determination, yet with a kind of half smile. When Demetria took a full look at him, she couldn't turn away. When he caught her eye, she blushed.

"This is the man you spurn, daughter," Istocles began, but Nauarchus put up his hand.

"Please," he said. "May I, my father?"

Istocles shook his head, but motioned for him to go forward.

"Clear the room, please," said Nauarchus. "This is between me and Demetria."

He had said her name! She had to admit, it sounded good coming from him.

Everyone filed out to wait on the front porch. Demetria hated to think what they would say, and hoped they would not listen at the door.

When they were all gone, he turned to her and said, "Are you all right?"

Demetria looked down at her dirty, snagged dress and nodded.

"I know this wedding is not your wish. I have a sister your age who is like you. I was told you were spirited, and I thought, at least I will have a wife who is like Thalassopoteia. I have loved and cherished her all my life."

"Oh," said Demetria, and wiped her face. More makeup came off. She looked down at her gray, greasy fingers.

"I have told my Thalassopoteia that the gods choose our lives for us, and we must obey them. But when I see you like this, my heart cannot but tell me-- Demetria, choose what you will. If you will not have me, I will go back to Massalia and marry another. I will endure the anger of your father and mine. I honor you, Demetria, in the name of shining Thalassopoteia."

Demetria could not believe her ears. "How... how... how did you know I'd be here?" she asked.

"Your parents complained that you liked to run away, and that no punishment would stop you. I simply asked to where you liked to run. I am sorry that your sweetheart has had a curse laid on him--"

"He's not. I mean to say, excuse me, sir, but he's not my sweetheart."

"--and I hope someday he will come to his right mind. But he is also a prince, so I hear."

"Yes, and a priest of Rome."

Nauarchus smiled. "I'm afraid you are a bit like Penelope."

"How is that?"

"You have a suitor whom you don't want, and a husband, or at least one that you wish to be your husband, who is far from you."

"Do you know our stories, then?" Demetria asked. Most Greeks knew the myth of Odysseus coming home from war after twenty years to his wife Penelope, and how many men had come around her while he was gone, to convince her he was dead, and to get her to marry one of them. But Massalia was so far away from Greece, Demetria thought perhaps they had forgotten.

"Of course. I have been known to sing them. I learned the songs of Homer in school, starting when I was very young."

"You are very accomplished. Someone said you know the

seas better than Poseidon."

"By that god, I hope not! He would be very jealous, I think."

"How old are you?"

"Not yet twenty-two years. Soon I will be, however."

"And yet you come into your father's property?"

"Father has much property to manage. We have been blessed by the gods in trading the resources of the land. When the seas are hospitable, we fill up our treasure houses, thank the gods."

Demetria had run out of questions, and still, this young, handsome man was standing near her, ready to listen. And in her mind's eye, there was Lucius, too, not as tall or as formed as a man, but full of passion for saving Rome, full of passion for her, and she for him.

Nauarchus folded his arms, saying nothing, and Demetria finally could stand the silence no longer. "Well, I suppose it is time for you to tell them."

"And what should I tell them?"

"As you said. That you don't want to marry me. That you are going home to Massalia and will marry another."

"No, no, Demetria." Nauarchus' eyes were tender and warm. "I didn't say that is what I would do. I said that if you didn't want me, then I wouldn't take you."

Demetria sighed, trying not to look directly at her fiancé. "You are too kind to me. You should do what you want."

"And yet."

Demetria stubbed one toe against the other, and pulled a stray twig from her dress. "By Hercules, are you going to make me decide?"

"Yes, by all the gods."

"Well," she said, and stole a look at him. A thought formed in her head that had the name Lucius in it, but she found herself pushing that away. It was too much. He was a prince. What were the possibilities? And what did she have now, at her feet? Too much, too much! If only. But he, Nauarchus. And Lucius. But not Lucius. If only.

Suddenly she blurted something that she did not know was coming. "I wonder," she said, and then shook her head, but went on. "If you would stay for a time. And talk to me again like this."

"I will stay, while our boat is repaired and we negotiate new agreements with our Roman friends. But soon I must go. Do you understand?"

"Yes," said Demetria. "Soon you must go." And she looked up into his eyes for the first time, and lost herself in them.

::VIII::

"I think you will need to explain yourself, my Lucius," Gallia was saying.

"Shhh! Not now, nurse," said Lucius. "I cannot hear."

"But you--"

"*Hist!*" Lucius burst out, and threw his arm down at her.

Gallia exchanged glances with Gnaeus, who shrugged his shoulders.

Lucius bent his ear toward the heavy door that separated the back of the house from the front. "Too thick," he said, half to himself. He cracked the door just a bit. "They have brought in Nauarchus, the man you said is betrothed to Demetria," Lucius whispered. "Wait a moment. Now they are all leaving. It is just she and the sailor."

"Master Lucius, I--" Gnaeus began.

Lucius put up his finger at Gnaeus and continued listening. "Keep the slaves away, if any remain in the back of the house."

Gnaeus glanced back, but he knew the whole household

was now on the front porch, except for them.

"I can't make it out," said Lucius.

"I think they are speaking Greek, my Lucius," said Gallia.

"They are speaking Greek. I think, I thought I heard. Something about Penelope. I wish I had listened better at my lessons."

Gallia shook her head, and put her arms over her chest.

"They are leaving. He is opening the door for her. That's it."

"We need to get you back to your room, master," Gnaeus said. "Before someone else finds out."

"What did they say?" Lucius wondered, tapping his fist against his chin.

"Master..." Gnaeus said.

Gallia said, "This deception. My Lucius, what do you have in mind?"

Lucius turned to them. "Let us go back to my room. There is much to be done."

No sunlight crept through the space between the shutter and the window in Lucius' bedroom. They lit lamps and talked by the light of them.

"I am sorry, dear nurse," Lucius began. "I had hoped to keep you out of this. But Demetria is so important."

"For what? I thought you had left all your childhood adventure behind," Gallia said. "You are a priest of Numa. And we were not supposed to see you for months, when the king said he would decide where you would go, the army, or back to--"

"Much has happened," Lucius said. "I have learned much. Much I cannot explain. Much I still do not understand. But I do know that I-- we-- must act. I must contact Demetria. We have a task."

"For what end?" Gallia said.

"To give Rome back to Romans," said Lucius.

"But you are Etruscan, too," Gallia cried out.

"It is too long to explain here," said Lucius. "Will you help me to speak to Demetria? In all likelihood we need to leave together, tonight, for our best chance of finishing our task."

"Task?" Gallia said.

"We must go to the Etruscan Land of the Dead, and retrieve Numa's second *baculum*. Unless we want the *haruspices* to destroy the shrine, keep the staffs, and assure that Rome will no longer be Rome, but Etruria, till the end of days."

"My Lucius, I cannot believe--"

"Dear nurse, I have to ask you to hold your tongue about all this. About my being a simpleton, and about my mission. If anyone finds out, we will fail."

"Is this just part of your condition of mind?" Gallia said. "If you are in your right mind, why are you speaking such nonsense?"

"Please, just promise me, you won't tell. At least not now. You have nothing to gain from telling, for if what I say are the words of an addlepate, then nothing will come of them. But if I am in my right mind, and I ask you a favor, you would be helping an old friend in need."

"He makes sense, lady," said Gnaeus.

"All right," Gallia said, and sighed.

"Now, can you arrange a meeting with Demetria, my nurse?"

"There is the possibility. Tomorrow night, we have the

procession of the Shield Dance. There will be a great crowd; farmers and shepherds will enter the city-- your cousins, from nearby towns as well."

Lucius slapped a fist on his palm. "The Shield Dance! Of course. The Dance of the Salian priests, the ones who leap! I did not realize the day was so close."

"Yes, there will be a great commotion. There will be paraders, shouting, and music, and the fearful banging on the shields with sticks. There might be a way to steal a quiet moment amidst the din. But Demetria will be watched closely. It is not like before. She is to be a bride, my Lucius."

"Not if I can help it," said Lucius. "And not if she can help it, either."

::IX::

The following sunset gave birth in Rome to the lights of hundreds of blazing torches. All along the Via those torches lined up, visible from the Capitoline where the Junius family lived.

It was the night of the Shield Dance of the Salian Priests, one of the holiest of the year.

Gallia managed to persuade Lucius' father and mother that Lucius should be allowed to see the procession, "To help him remember his former life." Gnaeus should come, too, she said, since he had never seen the Dance before.

Lucius, listening from outside the doorway, rejoiced when he heard his mother say, "All right, Gallia. But if he is terrified with the banging of the staffs on the shields, you must bring him home immediately!"

"Yes, mistress," said Gallia. "Of course, mistress."

"Thank you, my nurse!" cried Lucius later as he embraced her.

Meanwhile, Nauarchus and his crew were gathered in the

courtyard of Demetria's house. He, for his part, had persuaded Demetria's parents to let her go out with him and the family to watch the procession.

"She is pleasing to me," he said, "and it would give me no more pleasure than to be seen with her."

Istocles frowned. "This is not Greek," he said. "To have a man and woman out together, and they are not married."

"But you are Roman as well," Nauarchus reminded him. "And the Roman women, so I am told, will crowd the streets."

"They will not be outdone by the Etruscans," said Eodice. "These women by far outstrip their men in power."

Istocles shot Eodice a hard glance, but she was right. Etruscan women were much freer than Roman or Greek.

Demetria had listened to the whole conversation. She knew her father would say yes, because who could say no to this prince of merchants? She hoped they would be able to have a word amongst themselves only; he had listened so well before. She wanted that again. Could she tell him the truth about Lucius? Could he be part of their plan, their mission? Or would he be interested only in his sailing, his trading, and his sister far away in Massalia?

Or maybe it was much too soon to be thinking about telling secrets to someone she hardly knew.

Questions! Demetria thought to herself. *And no answers.*

Yet.

All the Greek women of Istocles' household went to the procession that night, closely wrapped in heavy wool dresses, with their heads covered. Since it was a cool night, Demetria willingly wrapped herself in the clothes of a grown woman and walked with Phane and the others, and her heart leapt at walking next to Nauarchus, who had put on a knee-length cloak to keep warm. The spitting torches gave uncertain light, so that at times, for the blink of an eye, Nauarchus would disappear into the night, and then come back again, look over at her, and smile.

At first, Nauarchus said that he would walk at her pace and stay with the women, but she clutched his arm and said she could keep up. And so they walked at the pace Nauarchus set, halfway between the women, and halfway between the men.

When they came to the Via, crowds had already formed, so they spent some time trying to find a place with few enough people that they could stand with a view of the coming dancers.

"You will see," Father was telling Nauarchus. "We also have a place in this ceremony, as do the Etruscans. King Numa began this tradition, so the story goes. He was the king after the first king, Romulus."

"I know of Numa," said Nauarchus. "For he touches on the history of Massalia as well. It is a story our ancestor Protus told us."

"Ah, I should like to hear the whole of it," Istocles said. "When the time comes."

The Junius family had taken their places on a wooden grandstand at the foot of the Capitoline Hill, constructed for the families who lived in that neighborhood.

"The procession begins away over there, my Gnaeus," Gallia was saying as he pointed to their right. "Just outside the north gate, where soldiers sometimes practice their spear- and sword-work."

"They will enter through the north gate," Marcus the elder

said, "then go by the Greek neighborhood and the vegetable market, then down by the Palatine Hill, where the king's people will watch, and then double back along the Via to our hill, the Capitoline, thence up the hill to the new temple that is being built."

Lucius knew that at the proper time Gallia could walk unseen along the parade route from the Capitoline to the Greek district. The light from the torches hid faces, and many unfamiliar people were in town. There were women and men out that night, and children ran free in the street if they were allowed-- and sometimes if they were not.

"Where is Marcus the younger?" Gnaeus asked, his eyes wider than even their usual roundness showed them. "I should think he will want to watch as well."

"It is well with Marcus," said Father. "It is well with him, young Lucius. Do you not remember?"

Lucius remembered. Marcus was one of the Salii, but it was unlawful to reveal the names of the dancers.

Gnaeus looked puzzled, but the elder Marcus quickly changed the subject. "One day, long ago, a shield fell from the sky." He used his left hand as the shield and made it fall into his right palm. "It was brought to Numa, our king, who interpreted it as a sign from the gods that Rome would someday be a great and lasting and city, shielded by the gods. He was instructed by his patroness, Egeria, to preserve the shield, and for as long as it was safe, so the city of Rome would be also."

Shielded by the gods, thought Lucius. *And with the baculum as well, no one could touch Rome.*

"To protect the shield when it was displayed, Numa had a

master craftsman named Mamurius create eleven other shields just like it. No one can tell the difference."

In the Greek neighborhood, Demetria listened as Istocles told Nauarchus the Greek version of the story. It was thrilling to be out with the men; the evening breeze seemed to quicken her and make her blood run faster.

And to have Nauarchus standing next to her-- well, her heart was big with pride. She couldn't help but think of Odysseus, the heroic seafarer, handsome and resourceful, when she looked up at Nauarchus. She had to remind herself that, of course, she wouldn't live with him on a ship when they married.

And who wants to live on a ship, anyway! she thought. Ugh, even to think of seasickness made her queasy.

But still and all...

"A long time ago," Istocles was saying, "a shield fell from the sky, so beautifully shaped that it must have been made by a god. It was brought to Numa, who interpreted it as a sign from Zeus (the Romans call him Jupiter), the king of the sky and of all mortals, to remember the story of his birth."

Demetria leaned in to hear the story Istocles told. She'd heard it from Phane before, but from a man's mouth it seemed new.

"As a baby, Jupiter had been hidden from his father Cronus, who feared that one of his offspring would overthrow him. Cronus had swallowed every one of Jupiter's siblings as babies, in order to keep them under his control. But when Jupiter was born, Rhea gave Cronus a stone wrapped in infant clothes and blankets. The silly god believed the stone was Jupiter, and swallowed it. Meanwhile, Rhea went to the island of Crete, south of Greece, and to a cave on a mountaintop, where she kept Jupiter until he was old enough to fend for himself.

"To muffle the cries of the baby, special helpers rallied around Rhea, called the Curetes. They were warriors and dancers who paraded about the cave, banging their swords against their shields. No one could hear baby Jupiter crying for his mother. The Curetes saw to that."

Baby crying for his mother, thought Demetria. That was what she would do when she was Nauarchus' wife-- stay at home and raise a little Zeus. How she hated babies screaming. But if she could have a little one like Phane's Nausimache! She was never any trouble.

"It is well to have a large family, as you do, father," said Nauarchus.

"Even so! May the gods protect us," said Antimachus.

"But you were saying..."

"Yes. Numa had had created eleven other shields like the one that fell from the sky, and he gave them and the magic one to the Salii, commanding them every year to remember the long-ago days of Jupiter's birth. This year, the celebration is to be even more important, for King Tarquinius has begun construction of a new temple on the Capitoline Hill, in the Greek style, with marble pillars in front, and it will be to Jupiter, whom they called Greatest and Best-- Optimus Maximus."

"The pipers! The pipers!" The crowd around the Istocles family cried.

A group of Etruscans musicians in short cloaks, their legs bare and gooseflesh in the cooling evening air, led the Salii into the city. Their instruments were both flutes and double pipes, and with them a number of young men in brightly-dyed cloaks also danced.

"These Etruscans call this music?" someone in the crowd said.

"The old ways aren't the same anymore," said someone else.

Istocles said, "The Etruscans must always be first in everything. The Salii are right behind them. You will see."

He was right. The procession of high-born Roman men could be heard before they appeared in the torch light, carrying heavy staffs and long, oval shields that tapered towards their middles. The shields glinted in the torchlight, highly polished and bound in leather.

Bronze helmets with crowns like cones sat on the young men's heads. Masks made of leather were fixed to the inside of the helmet with nails. Eyeholes, with brows and lashes carefully dyed around their edges, decorated the masks, and the leather dangled down in individual strips, suggesting beards.

There were twelve of them, with six on a side. They turned, teetered on one leg, and then leaped again and banged the shields. The ones on the right went first, then the other six mirrored their movements.

In years past, when the shield dancers came by, Demetria would follow them, darting in and out between the legs of the other spectators, running after Lucius and the other Roman boys. Seeing the young men dressed in warrior gear, helmets with masks, leaping up and bashing the bronze shields with their wooden staffs was exciting, but it was even more so to make her own kind of procession, to see all the different kinds of people along the route, to go into different neighborhoods at night, to cheer and whoop and scream and make her own dances.

But all that was behind her now. She was a woman, wrapped in a woman's long dress and head covering, and she was with her future husband. Suddenly she longed to run again, even in that dress that kept her legs from reaching their full stride. But she looked up at Nauarchus again, he smiled back, and she linked her arm around his.

And she no longer felt the wind.

The shields were the most interesting part of the dancers' equipment. They were identical and made of bronze, highly polished so that they were as bright as a new tin pot, wide at the top and bottom, thinner in the middle. The dancers held the shields at their thin middle with leather handles. At the top and bottom were intricate designs, lines that looked like letters and writing but weren't. And there were pictures that looked like the heads of animals, though Demetria couldn't be sure what kind. She had not seen the shields close enough to tell, and every year the torch light served more to make the shields shine and glint rather than revealing what was on their surface.

Now, as Demetria stood there and the dancers leapt and clashed, then changed places, stepping in rhythm, she really looked at the shields, looked until her eyes hurt. She still couldn't quite make out what was on them, and she turned away, for the reflection from the shields flared and made spots before her eyes.

The priests chanted as they danced, in Latin that was older than that spoken in Rome:

Jupiter, bringer of light! All the earth trembles at the sound of your thunder!

After this line, the priests would beat the metal of the shield, imitating the noise that came from Jupiter's sky.

"Cover your ears," Nauarchus said to Demetria, who laughed and leaned close to him, rejoicing in his warmth and sturdy limbs.

"*Cozuelodorieso!*" The priests cried over and over, in between the verses of the song.

Demetria had never known what these words meant, but children often chanted it when they played at procession, and now and then would say instead, "*casus de caelestiis!*" *The shield fallen from the heavenly gods.*

"We also have our part," said Istocles, and pointed. In the distance there came a costumed party: one was dressed as the goddess Rhea, the mother of Zeus, pulling a little cart tricked out to look like a baby's cradle. In the cradle an actual baby lay wrapped up tightly, attended by young girls. Behind the mother and child was a huge man, Saturn, with a big belly, and behind him, five Greek children who were the immortal brothers and sisters of baby Jupiter. The last child pulled a cart with a big black stone in it.

"There is no reason for this Greek stuff," someone next to Demetria said.

Demetria was about to tug on the person's cloak and set them straight, but she felt a tug on her own dress. Outside the torchlight, someone was motioning to her. "Excuse me," she said to Nauarchus. "Here is one who wishes to speak to me."

"Let her come forward," said Nauarchus. "She can speak to all of us."

"You don't understand," said Demetria.

"Go, I understand," said Nauarchus, and turned away. As the procession had passed, the crowds were falling in line to follow.

Gallia, Lucius' nurse, took hold of her arm, and Demetria put her hand over Gallia's hand.

"Lady Demetria," she began.

"No, let it be Demetria, good nurse," she said. "I am not married yet."

"My child!" Gallia embraced her. "Both of you have grown so in so little time!" Her cheek touched Demetria's, and it was wet.

"What is it?"

"Lucius," she said. "He has frightened me with this deception. He speaks of a mission to keep Rome for the Romans, but I do not understand. He wishes me to give you this message: *Come to me tonight, after the procession, for we leave for the Etruscan Land of the Dead.*"

"Etruscan Land of the Dead! What does he mean? Where is this place?"

"I know nothing about it, only that he thinks he must go there with you."

Demetria looked back toward the street. She could still see Nauarchus, a head taller than anyone else in the crowd, but he was getting father away moment by moment.

This is too fast, she thought. *Nauarchus is here for only a short time, and--*

"Must it be tonight?" Demetria said.

"Lucius said it must," Gallia said.

Demetria craned her neck to see the head of Nauarchus, still visible, but even farther away now. "I have a guest,"

Demetria said finally. "I can't leave him now."

"It is true, my dear." Gallia took Demetria's hand. "You are speaking sense, as I knew you would. You are a good Greek girl with a good head on your shoulders."

"Speaking sense?"

"Yes, child! You have a future to think of with a handsome husband. Think of the children you will have with him!"

"Children?" Suddenly Demetria thought of baby Zeus-- and realized he had five brothers and sisters.

"Of course. You must think of the family who will be your comfort in old age. You want to have strong sons who will keep safe the property that your husband will give them, after he has retired from his seafaring."

"Children?"

"Yes, don't sound so surprised. You will have them in good time, if the gods allow."

Demetria again looked back toward Nauarchus. *It is well to have a large family*, he'd said. She knew little about how women became pregnant, but she knew very well what it was like for a woman to give birth. It was difficult, full of pain, and she knew of young wives who had died of it, for news traveled fast in the Greek neighborhood of Rome. Would she have to do so over and over again?

Suddenly, adventure with Lucius became much more attractive.

"Tell him I will be there," said Demetria.

Gallia stared, but Demetria embraced her one last time and pushed her gently away. "Go, dear nurse. Please."

Gallia disappeared into the night.

When Demetria rejoined Nauarchus, he said, "Is all well

with your Lucius?"

"It wasn't Lucius. But I think you are very clever, like Odysseus."

Nauarchus smiled. "That is the nickname my Thalassopoteia gave me."

"I feel I know her already, you speak of her so often," Demetria said in her best innocent-sounding voice.

Nauarchus seemed not to notice her tone. "You and she will be great friends. By Athena. You are very like each other."

Demetria turned away for a moment, suddenly cold, and thought *He cannot be interested in me. It is Thalassopoteia he is thinking of. I don't know how I ever--*

But before she could let her spirit enlarge that idea, someone in the street caught her eye. There, on the side of the street in front of a booth selling sausages, stood one of the *haruspices* that had come to Portentia the year before. It was Repsuna, bald and bug-eyed. There was no mistaking his face, but it was clear he didn't want to be recognized. He was wearing a long cloak and a hat with a low brim, like a traveler's. There were many such with hats like these, for travelers came from outside Rome to watch the Salii. But a *haruspex* normally wore hats like cones, and Repsuna was a resident of Rome. He hadn't had far to travel.

Repsuna continued on with the procession, walking slowly behind it, and in and out of the crowd, until he was gone.

"Strange!" Demetria cried out loud, and then put her hand over her mouth.

"What is strange?" Nauarchus asked.

"Nothing!" Demetria was quick to say. "It's just that... I can never tell exactly what is on those shields."

"They are of the gods."

"Yes," said Demetria, and allowed herself a long look at Nauarchus. How kind he was to stay with her, when he could be with all his crew and the men of Demetria's family!

I can't marry you, she began to say to herself, but then thought better of it. *At least, not until we have finished our mission.*

::X::

Once the procession left the Greek neighborhood, Istocles instructed all the women to go back home; the men would follow and attend the ceremony on the Capitoline Hill next to the temple under construction. Priests known as *flamines* would sacrifice animals once the procession arrived at the top of the hill, and at midnight, the king would address the people.

Demetria bit her tongue instead of protesting to be allowed to see all this, and she bade farewell to Nauarchus. As she and the rest of the women retraced their steps home, Demetria looked back often, until Phane remarked that Demetria must be very taken with her fiancé.

But Demetria was hoping to pick out Repsuna in the torchlight.

An endless half-hour went by while Phane and the others made ready for bed. Hardly had Phane begun her nightly snoring than Demetria was out of the house, wrapped tightly in a cloak and tight-fitting woven wimple, a kind of cap, running quickly to Lucius'.

This time she did not need to take back ways, for the darkness and the still crowded streets gave her cover. She kept on thinking of Repsuna and wondered what he must have be up to, but her primary thought was of Lucius.

It wasn't long before she had an answer of a kind. As she came near to the foot of the Palatine Hill, she caught sight not only of Repsuna, but Turanquil herself, the *haruspica* with the scar on her face from the wound she received when Lucius had thrown the *baculum* at her mirror.

They stood next to a stand of benches, under a pole with a torch attached. Turanquil was dressed as most women that night, in a long dress with a head scarf. But she was also wearing a veil that covered her mouth. The veil puffed outwards as she spoke with Repsuna, quick, tense puffs of air that indicated she was speaking quickly and sharply to her colleague. She was also gesticulating, pointing this way and that, and Repsuna was nodding.

Demetria slowed her pace, then stopped in front of the now empty grandstand, and watched the two *haruspices* as they spoke. There were fewer people milling about, so she took a place behind the tiered benches, redolent of new pine resin.

Soon the two seers were joined by a third, again one of the men who had come to Portentia, named Velthur. After speaking for a moment, they walked off down the street and away from the Palatine.

Demetria decided to follow them.

They headed along a street that would take them to the Via and from there toward the Capitoline Hill, the way the Salii had taken, and on the way to Lucius' house. Demetria would be able to meet Lucius in good time if the seers kept going that direction, but even if not, she considered it important to know what the Etruscans were doing. She had worn good, sturdy sandals with leather thongs that tied at the ankle, just in case the Etruscan Land of the Dead required a long walk, so adding another few paces to the night would not be difficult.

Lucius, Demetria thought, would probably thank her that she had investigated this secret meeting, and maybe it would help them on whatever journey they must take.

The *haruspices* threaded their way between bands of dancers imitating the Salii. The boom of drums echoed throughout the dark city, and Etruscan pipes played high above the deep booming. When they reached the Via, the trio of seers quickened their pace noticeably. Demetria's sandals slapped smartly on the stone-paved street.

Soon the Via and the Forum were left behind, and the path began to rise. The Capitoline Hill was wreathed in torchlight. Demetria's eyes were dazzled every time she looked up at it, and she took to watching the stride of her sandaled feet to keep spots from filling her eyes.

The Etruscans continued up the hill, and the street began to curve and switch back with the increased steepness of the grade. The crowds were greater here, because the Salii were nearly on top of the hill, and the king was going to speak from the steps of the temple he was having constructed.

Now and then Demetria had to push through a group of revelers, and it was lucky she met no one she knew. The *haruspices* had no such trouble, for the crowds parted as they made their swift way, not running and yet not walking either.

"Maybe they have to be on the hill for a religious ceremony," Demetria said to herself, beginning to be out of breath. "Maybe they think they are late."

But halfway up the hill, there was a fork in the street. One way went up to the temple area, and the other to the residential area and the Junius family home. The *haruspices* turned left, toward the houses.

Soon after they turned, however, they slipped down an alleyway between two houses owned by important Romans. There was no crowd here, and Demetria had fallen behind in order not to be noticed. Demetria ran to the alley once they disappeared. It was now completely dark-- no light from the torches came this far, and though the night was clear, there was as yet no moon.

Demetria reached the alley and saw nothing but a black hole to nowhere. "Back to Lucius, then!" she said to herself, but hesitated, reluctant to leave the seers to whatever they were about to do.

That moment of hesitation made all the difference. Not far in front of her, first one, then two, then three tiny lights appeared, no doubt from hand-held oil lamps. Demetria paused to undo her sandals and take them off. She could not be seen outside the small circle of light that the lamps provided, but she certainly could be heard.

The *haruspices* soon made a right turn out of the alleyway into a garden, along a path that was beaten grass and dirt. The path was soft, fortunately, and the grass still green, so that it made little more than a whisper when pressed.

Taking that path, the follower and the followed had doubled back, and were facing straight toward the temple and the place where the Salii must be doing their final dances before the king's speech.

"They do not like crowds!" Demetria thought. "Even with their faces covered, they are not unseen enough!"

Not far away, light again came from the torches of the Roman revelers. But the *haruspices* kept to paths in the woods along the back of the Etruscans' houses, finally coming to a stop in a grove of wild olives and thorny bushes a short way from the temple precinct. There they extinguished their lamps, and huddled in a circle.

Demetria dropped into a crouch, and moved forward. Her aim was to get as close to the *haruspices* as possible-- to listen to their conversation, hear or see what they might do. The trio were silhouetted by the torchlight, though imperfectly so, because the thick undergrowth in the grove gave them good cover.

Still, Demetria was able to make it to within a few paces of them, before she stopped-- not because she could go no farther, but because of what the *haruspices* did: they all three took out the magic mirrors they had used to transport the spirits of people into another world.

The mirrors were bronze, and flashed briefly in the uncertain light. Turanquil, who happened to be taller than the men she was with, lifted the mirror up above her head. The oval disk was clearly outlined, first because of the distant torch light, but then because it made its own light-- it began to glow dull, then brighter orange, as if it were being heated in a blacksmith's fire.

In this glow, Demetria could now make out the other two figures, who were facing each other, kneeling, and holding their mirrors out horizontally next to each other and with the disks parallel to the ground. It almost looked as if they were holding fry pans over an outdoor fire, except that the "fire" was coming from above: the glow of Turanquil's mirror was now lighting the other two seers' mirrors as well.

The light made a triangle between the mirrors that gradually brightened from dim gray to bright orange. And of a sudden, the light flared into a ball that, in one motion the *haruspices* cast into the sky.

The sphere flew up high above the hill and exploded with a bang.

The entire area was lit up orange, as if it were on fire. The people gasped, then screamed. But the *haruspices* were not finished. They quickly created a second ball of fire, cast it into the sky, and it exploded in a hail of sparks that fell among the crowd in pinks and reds.

Demetria, who had been kneeling, cast herself fully on the ground. The *haruspices* had been careful not to make the fireballs explode over them, and in the grove it was still dark, but Demetria was more frightened than thinking of concealing herself.

The crowd also was frightened. They began to run down the street from the temple in a mass amid screams and roars of dismay. Then something made them stop.

Demetria lifted her head at the sudden quiet. The Etruscans were still in the grove, focusing their mirrors in a triangle, and now, within that space, Demetria saw a picture made of light. It was of a female face-- or a mask of a female face, for there were no eyes, only black holes. The face did not have hair, but snakes grew out of her scalp, with licking tongues. Behind the face flared a set of fiery wings, flapping as a bird's.

The face then seemed to speak-- its full lips moved-- but no sounds came, except for a kind of hissing that was a combination of a snake's and of steam coming from a boiling, covered cook pot.

This was enough to instill panic in everyone, including Demetria. She screamed, scrambled up and away, using a hand on the ground to steady herself as she rushed back down the path from where she had come. She clutched her sandals and didn't look back.

Down the alleyway she ran barefoot and made a left turn back toward the street that would take her down the hill and back home. She had no thought at all but somehow to get away from the hissing face with the snakes and wings.

When she returned to the main street, she could go no farther, for the crowd coming from the temple stopped her in her tracks. If she tried to get into the pack of sprinting men, she would surely be overrun and trampled. She stopped and looked up, and the face was still there, towering over the top of the hill.

But something had changed.

Another source of light now shined at the top of the hill, and the light was focused in a beam up at the face. Demetria stared, opened her eyes wider, glanced at the pack of people still running with all their might down the hill, then looked again. Something on the ground was shining brighter than torches, brighter even than the image of the goddess monster in the sky.

Demetria, suddenly heartened, scrambled up onto a rock wall next to the street that made a border between the street and the house on the corner. The height gave her a somewhat better view of the light on the ground, but she would have to get a lot closer to see what it exactly was.

The light was now boring a hole in the image in the sky-- it was like a long spear or log, a beam of strong brilliance, and the image in the sky was fading.

Demetria stepped over the rock wall into the garden of the house, and made her way up several stone terraces with stick fences bound together with twine. Her hand trailed over grass and wildflowers that had grown there through the rainy winter. She stepped into a puddle, and a shock went through her from toe to scalp. Still she ran back up the hill, now out of the garden, through a line of trees, and into an open area, just in front of the stone boundaries that market the temple precinct.

Here she could see what was happening-- no one was left on top of the hill except a few men. The Salian priests were standing firm, the tapered ovals of their shields in front of them for protection. Farther away, the king stood on the porch of the unfinished temple with a few assistants.

The light came from one shield. The other eleven only reflected what was already there.

"The shield of Numa!" Demetria whispered. "There is no way Rome will be defeated!"

Indeed, it seemed that the light from the shield was now stronger than ever, and the image in the sky weaker. The image now seemed more like colored smoke than a face, and the Salian priest who held the shield was working it this way and that, so that its beam of light fell on every area of what had once been a terrifying prodigy.

Suddenly, there was a flaring of light from the grove where the Etruscans had hidden. It was brief, but easily seen, like a flame that flares for a second and is extinguished. Perhaps the

Etruscans were readying another fire ball, but they had lost the element of invisibility.

Many of the Salii cried out and pointed. The Salian priest with the shield of Numa pulled down the shield from its position over his head and focused it at the grove. A strong light reflected back at him, and he began to run toward it.

"The light! To the light!" He yelled to his brothers, and they all began to converge on the grove.

Demetria found herself running again. She had to warn the Salian priests! If they shined the shield light at the mirrors of the haruspices, it was likely to reflect back at him and do whatever harm he intended for his enemies. She wished to cry out but found her throat too dry and her voice cracking.

The Salian with the shield disappeared into the grove, but his fellows did not follow him. There was a flash of light, so bright it blinded everyone for a moment.

Demetria put her hands in front of her eyes. The mirrors! The *haruspices* must have used their mirrors to reflect the shield's light back at the priest. She changed course and made for the grove. How could she help? All she could see was popping flashes of brilliance.

Once in the grove, she knelt and let the glow from the flash fade. When her vision came clear again, she could easily see, in the pools of light made of mirrors and the shield, the *haruspices* in a knot on one side, and the Salian priest on the other. He had taken off his mask and was shaking his head, kneeling and leaning on the shield, which was still between him and the seers.

Demetria strained her eyes. The face on the Salian-- it was Marcus the Younger.

Turanquil spoke. "Roman. Leave the shield and go."

Marcus had been hurt. He didn't answer, only shook his head and rubbed his eyes. Demetria crept closer and gasped-- blood was dripping from one of Marcus' eyes.

"The shield!" Repsuna now said. "Give it, and retain your life."

Marcus took his hands from his eyes. Both were bleeding. "No," he rasped. "Never." And he managed to stand up and bring the shield to his chest.

What can I do? Demetria thought. She stood up. "Your mirrors!" she cried, as if in a dream. It was a cracking, weak voice.

The *haruspices* turned and caught sight of her.

"Here," she called, and waved her arms.

Her plan should have worked. The *haruspices* all brought their mirrors up to Demetria and lost sight of Marcus for a moment. But Marcus stumbled, set his palm on the ground, pivoted on it, and hesitated. He could not see. If he could, he would have fled straight out of the grove.

As it was, he had turned the shield far enough away from the seers that he was an easy target for a knife in the back. Someone threw it-- Demetria could not tell who-- and it struck Marcus with a thump, making him pitch forward. His hands went to his back to try to pull it out, and he let the shield fall on the ground.

At Turanquil's bidding, the other two seers ran for Marcus. One picked up the shield, and the other stabbed Marcus again.

That was all Demetria saw. As another dagger whistled by her ear, she ran like she had never run before.

::XI::

Even before Demetria could make the familiar nine taps on Lucius' shutter, the silence of the night made it easy to hear her arrive, out of breath, her sandals tramping on the tall spring grass. Lucius opened the shutter, got her attention with a whispered hiss, and arranged to meet her in their secret shrine. He carried an oil lamp there, and was careful to hold his hand between the flame and the late evening breeze that was coming up from the coast.

When they arrived at the place, a thicket of bushes that made a natural shelter, they crawled in through the parting between two slender trunks. They had seldom gone into the place at night, and even with the lamplight, it seemed strange, as if other children had used it long ago. There was a clay table that was the shrine to the God of Everything, the deity they had decided was their protector, and a large pile of leaves of bark on which they had written their sacred script, playing at priest of Numa and handmaid.

They embraced on their knees; the shelter wasn't tall

enough for them to stand, and for the longest time they had simply sat cross-legged when they were in it. Demetria was still out of breath, and with their arms around each other her panting warmed Lucius' ear. It was the longest that they had ever held each other, and Lucius regretted that they had been apart so long.

"I'm sorry I couldn't tell you sooner," he said when they let each other go. "The *haruspices*--"

"--have attacked, they've stolen--" Demetria said.

"would have killed me for sure--"

"--the shield of Numa!"

"What?"

"Killed?"

"Start over! Calm down!" They both said together, and Lucius took Demetria's hands. How changed they were! Lucius thought well and truly that everything they had known before was gone. And Demetria was to be married. What could he do about it?

"I'm trying to say that I didn't want to deceive you," he said, giving her hand a squeeze. It felt cold and was soiled with dirt, almost as if she had dipped it in a mud puddle. "Your hands. Where were you?"

She took her hand away from his and rubbed it in the other. "It's because I was there. I mean, it's the *haruspices*. They--"

"They what?"

"The *haruspices* have stolen the Shield of Numa. And--" she hesitated, and brought her hand to her eyes.

"And?" He stared at Demetria in the paleness of the lamplight. What was happening? Something was very wrong, but he couldn't imagine what.

Demetria wiped an eye. It was clear she was crying, but her voice, for now, was steady. "Gallia gave your message to me, and I was coming to see you."

"And I was up waiting for you."

"But I'd noticed a *haruspex* following the procession-- Repsuna. He was alone at first, but then met up with Turanquil, and finally the other one--"

"Velthur."

"Right. Velthur joined them, and they headed to the Capitoline Hill. They hid in a grove next to the Temple of Jupiter on the Capitoline."

"Did you see the prodigy-- the face of the goddess?"

"Yes, did you?"

"Yes, but I wasn't there with the Salii. Mother decided it would be upsetting to me, the simpleton, to be out so late in such great crowds, and Father agreed."

Demetria nodded vigorously. "Parents!"

"But I wanted to be part of the celebration somehow-- we had always done so, hadn't we-- and so I opened my window and climbed out onto the roof of the house. I think that window must be getting smaller, or I am getting bigger, for it was truly difficult to squeeze out this time."

"How many times we lay on our backs on that roof!" Demetria whispered. "The thatch of that second floor was like a bed to lie on, so different from the tiles of the main house!"

"Summer nights!" Lucius said, and took her hand again. They had gone up there together just to watch shooting stars and fill their eyes with the band of stars that was a trail of cream across the sky, when the evening breeze had carried away the haze of cooking fires.

Lucius wished they could go out there now, and forget about everything, even if just for a moment. But he forced himself to go on. The dread, the sense that something was wrong, drove him. "At first there was only the light of torches, but then, when the image of the goddess was thrown into the sky, it was as if the whole city was lit up. Then the light from the ground-- I couldn't see--"

"It was the true Shield," said Demetria. "Defending the city against the prodigy. But it did not come from beyond this world. The *haruspices* made it themselves with their mirrors. I saw them. I was crouching behind bushes, watching. I am the only one who knows."

"And now all the people have gone home. I lowered myself down. There is no revelry as there is normally. Something has happened."

Demetria nodded. "It is terrible. Lucius. I don't know how to--" She fell silent, and looked away.

Lucius' heart darkened and his stomach dropped.

Demetria spoke, all of it in one breath, it seemed. "When the Salian priests began to fight back against the prodigy, and the shield of Numa lit up and defeated the prodigy, they caught sight of the *haruspices* hidden in the grove. One of the priests, the one with the real shield, went into the grove with the shield. I went after him. I saw everything. That is why my hands are dirty. Lucius, I'm sorry. The priest. I saw him. It was your brother."

"Marcus?" Now the dread leapt from his stomach to his face. Demetria seemed to disappear. All he saw was mist.

"They killed him, Lucius, and they took the Shield."

"No," said Lucius, anger beginning to boil. "No. It wasn't him. Another had possession of the shield tonight. Someone else. It wasn't him."

"It was, Lucius. I tried to help. I tried to distract the *haruspices*. But he was already blinded from the mirror reflection."

"No!" Lucius screamed. He leaned forward, slapped his head on the ground. "No! Not my brother."

"I'm sorry, Lucius. I wish--"

"You didn't see him! It wasn't him!"

Demetria's tears rolled. "We need to avenge him, Lucius. We need to retrieve the Shield. Then the *baculum*. Once we have both, no one will be able to defeat us. We can avenge Marcus then."

"No! You don't speak anymore." Lucius thrust his hand into the fold of his tunic, brought out something and put it in Demetria's hand. It was a grammarstone.

"*Os Graecae clausa.*" The mouth of the Greek girl... closed.

Demetria put her hands to her throat. A gasping, choking sound came from it. Her lips moved, but nothing came out. Finally, her lips closed, and would not reopen. She could only manage a tiny squeak, but her eyes asked Lucius, unmistakably, *why?*

Lucius didn't know why. He wasn't thinking. He was too angry to think. But he said, "You are my handmaid. You will obey me."

Demetria threw the grammarstone at Lucius as hard as she could. The stone went off his forearm and into the branches of a bush. Then she leaned over, slapped Lucius in the face, crawled out of the shelter, and ran.

The blow cleared Lucius' head as if a great wind had come and cleared away the fog of his anger and disbelief. Suddenly he realized what he had done, and he regretted it.

"Demetria!" he called after her, rubbing his cheek. "Wait! At least let me undo the grammar!"

But she did not wait, and Lucius did not make a grammar that would stop her. He scrambled out of the shelter and thought about running after her, but he had no heart for it. She was right to run. He had never perfected a grammar against anyone he loved. She was speaking the truth. Of course she was! Her tears told him. But he had not wanted to admit it. Anything but that news! Anything but Marcus, dead.

Lucius lay on the floor of the shelter and wept. He wept for a long time, and the spirit of Marcus seemed to hover above him, asking to be let go. He wept until he could not feel the blow to his cheek anymore, until the pain had gone from his cheek deep into his heart.

Then a thought came to him. To avenge Marcus.

He stared at the tiny flame of the oil lamp, and considered what he should do.

There were a thousand grammars that would destroy the three *haruspices*. He needed to find them somehow, and before he killed them, he would need to tell them why he was killing them. And then, lightning. Or fire. Or something else.

But their mirrors.

As long as they had their mirrors.

And the Shield! They had that, as well.

It would be difficult.

Lucius' heart lifted as he walked back through the trees and the darkness on the path he knew so well. He didn't care how difficult it would be. He had the power of the grammarstones. Glyph had said he could do anything with them.

But with the *baculum*.

He stopped. In the distance, a nightingale called. Cicadas chanted in the trees. It was almost as if he had heard that word in Demetria's voice.

With the baculum, no one will defeat us.

With the *baculum*, he could destroy the *haruspices* easily. They would join Marcus in death, taking his message to his brother. *Lucius avenged you, warrior of Rome.* Then he could be king of Rome. Demetria could be queen. She would forget the Greek from Massalia. She would want to be with a powerful man, the most powerful in the world, as she had once said he would be.

Unless she preferred--

But he didn't say the name, and he didn't think anymore of him. He began to run.

He entered his house through the back door, hesitated, then made a right turn to go to the slave quarters. Gnaeus had preferred to sleep there when he wasn't allowed to make a bed outside Lucius' room in the upstairs hallway.

He tiptoed into the small room where three male slaves slept on low beds. He knelt at Gnaeus', and gently shook him till he woke.

"Master Lucius?"

Lucius put his hand gently over Gnaeus' mouth. He would never perfect another grammar against a friend. He motioned in the lamplight for Gnaeus to follow him.

They went upstairs, Gnaeus rubbing his eyes. When they were alone, Lucius said, "I must go to the Etruscan Land of the Dead now."

"But it's so late," said Gnaeus. "Maybe you should go in the morning, when it's light and you have rested."

"Dear Gnaeus," said Lucius. "I know you are not yet quite awake. I need you to help me. I need you to remember."

"Remember," said Gnaeus, and yawned.

Lucius found his bag of grammarstones. There may have been fifty in it, all the grammarstones he had. He took out a handful, closing them in his fist, not knowing exactly how many he had taken. He put them in Gnaeus' hand, and closed his over them. They vibrated and whirred, and Gnaeus startled.

"Grammarstones?" he said, suddenly much more awake than he had been. "But Lucius--"

"I need you to give these to Demetria," he said. "Please. I-- I had an argument with her. She must know. Know that we are partners. We are together, Gnaeus. We will always be together."

"The prodigy tonight. Are you going back to Logo to ask what you must do?"

"No, Gnaeus," said Lucius, putting his other hand over the first. "It's for my brother. I have to show I can. On my own. And it must be tonight, as soon as I can. But Gnaeus..."

"Yes, I am listening."

"The grammarstones. Find a way to give them to Demetria. Please. And when you have done that, you may go back to Portentia and the shrine before the haruspices can intercept you and make you tell them where it is. Tell Logo I am doing what he sent me to do."

"Yes, Master Lucius. It will be done."

"And Gnaeus--"

"Yes, Master Lucius?"

"May your genius go with you."

Gnaeus clasped Lucius' hand. "And yours with you."

::XII::

Demetria knew that the grammar Lucius had perfected would not last forever. To do that, he would have to have put the word *sempiterna* in the phrase. It was cold comfort. Her mouth felt as if it had been filled with itchy wool. She ran as much as she was able, then began to cough, and had to slow down.

Fresh tears came, and she wiped them away angrily, tears of shame and fatigue and disbelief. Could she have saved Marcus? If she had, the conversation with Lucius would have taken a different path. They might be together, making plans to retrieve the Shield.

At the same time, she hated Lucius for perfecting the grammar on her. How could he? You do not hurt those you love.

I was only the bringer of bad tidings. I did not kill Marcus.

By the time she reached her own neighborhood, Demetria's thoughts had turned to her family. She knew they would be worried about her, that they might be out looking for her. On the night of this prodigy, all parents would wish to have their children safely in their homes.

The house of Istocles was not asleep when she arrived. The gate to the courtyard was open, and a fire had been lit in a pit there. Roundabout, a group of men milled and talked.

She paused and hid herself next to the corner of a house. The voice of Istocles, and then Nauarchus, were unmistakable.

A slave was standing lookout just outside the gate, so she doubled back and approached the house from behind. She climbed the high stone wall that ringed the courtyard, careful to place her sandaled feet on protruding stones, and peeked over the top.

Istocles was warming his hands at the fire and speaking. "...send out slaves to search, if she's not back soon," he said. His concern was limned in the firelight, that characteristic fatherly frown of his. For a moment, Demetria regretted all the worry she had caused him over the years.

Nauarchus said, "By Hermes, she has had good luck with travel in the past. I pray she is safe. It is clear she knows every corner of the city."

One of Demetria's uncles spoke up. He lived nearby and had several sons present in the group of men. "My brother tells me you have a story about Massalia and King Numa. How can Greeks be interested in this Shield that all are talking about tonight? Speak."

Yes," said Istocles. "Speak. And if Demetria has not returned when you are finished, we will send out the slaves."

Nauarchus nodded. "You well know that our ancestors, the Phocaeans, founded Massalia three generations ago, when the king of Rome was Tarquinius Priscus, the grandfather of the present king. The story goes that our founder, Protus, swore an oath of friendship with Tarquinius-- who spoke not on behalf of Rome but for the Etruscans themselves, who had become masters of Rome."

Demetria admired Nauarchus' way of speaking. Though he was young, he was sure of himself, and stood up as an equal among older men.

"But Protus was approached secretly by a man of great importance, Titus Titurius, who urged him to repudiate his alliance with Etruria in favor of Rome, which he said someday would be a great nation. And as evidence Titurius gave the example of the great shield of Numa, which had fallen from the sky during Numa's reign. Protus was greatly interested in the shield, and asked if he could see it, for an artifact of the gods must be quite beautiful. Titurius said that he would be able to show Protus the twelve shields that the Salian priests dance with, but not the actual shield, so that the Etruscans would not be able to torture him and find the answer."

"I wonder that the Etruscans have not taken all twelve, and have done with it," said one of the uncles, Halitherses.

"Because they fear the gods?" said another.

Istocles made a sign to ward away the evil eye. "I am told the Etruscans did not steal the shields because the Romans hand-picked the Salians from the greatest athletes of the nobility, and they would not be able to catch all twelve at one time.

"Among our people, a different story is told." said Nauarchus. "When Protus was taken to the temple of to inspect the shields, Titurius revealed that there is one identifying mark on the shield that came from the sky, and that is a word of grammar somewhere on it, carefully hidden so that no one may see except those who think to look. It is written in the Latin language, and was an invention of Numa. This word of grammar, if spoken, would summon the shield to the one speaking it, taking it from the one who had stolen it. Therefore, no one could ever steal the shield and keep it, if there is someone who knows the word of grammar and can speak it properly."

"Did Titurius tell Protus the word?"

"Yes and no. Protus was so impressed by the beauty of all twelve shields-- so cunningly wrought that he could not tell the real one-- that he committed the Massalian people to secret friendship with the Romans forever. Titurius then told him, as a mark of trust, the secret name of the shield but not the full grammar that went with it."

"But the Romans must know what this missing grammar is," said Istocles. "They should be able to summon the shield at any time. Doubtless they have already done so!"

Nauarchus spread his hands, palms up. "Provided they also have the word of summoning. It has been many generations since Numa made that inscription, and maybe the lore has been lost."

"The lore is not lost, for Lucius Junius Brutus, Demetria's beloved, went to study it last year!" said the youngest uncle, Thalassocrates.

All turned to him and frowned, but Nauarchus said, "We will see if he is truly her beloved. If he is, perhaps she will not return tonight. A lady who is truly devoted to a man will not depart from him, simpleton or no."

Demetria blushed to her neck, though no one could see her. Devoted? After that grammar of silence? And he was not a simpleton, but he was not a man like Nauarchus. Nauarchus was the one who was truly wise, she thought. He had given her the key to returning the shield: the proper grammar, matched with the secret name of the shield. She would need to go back to Logo, and tell him the news. He would have the stones, and doubtless he would know the shield name and the grammar that went with it, for Numa would have had it safeguarded in the archives.

She would have to go that night, despite everything, and without Lucius. The grammar of silence had weakened in the time it had taken for Nauarchus to tell his story, but she still burned with fury when she thought of Lucius.

"Demetria!"

It was the voice of the lookout slave. He had made a circuit of the property, and seen her.

"Demetria! Come down from there! Your father wishes you home!"

The slave yelled as loud as he could on purpose. He knew that if she ran, he would not be allowed to touch her, and she might escape. But if the others knew, they could chase her down.

Shhh! You worthless thing! Demetria tried to say, but the wool feeling in her mouth stopped her from speaking, and she could only cough.

In a flash, there was Nauarchus, having run outside the courtyard by way of the gate. Demetria had not climbed down from the bottom of the wall before he was there, blocking her way. And many men came after him.

"Demetria!" Istocles cried when he saw her. "This will be the last time you ever get free." He ordered a slave to tell Eodice and the others who must also have been waiting in the women's' quarters.

Nauarchus shook his head, but when she looked up at him, he nodded and through his serious expression gave her a little half-smile.

"By Hercules!" Demetria gasped as her father took her by the arm. She was able to speak! The grammar had worn off, thanks be to the gods. She had only a moment to give Nauarchus a backward glance. Nothing came from her mouth, but not because of the grammar.

"Do you know how you made us worry?" said Eodice when Demetria was delivered to the back of the house. "All Rome is in peril! A prodigy was seen above the Capitoline Hill!"

"I know, mother!" said Demetria. "I am not simple like Lucius Junius Brutus."

And before Demetria had a moment to regret what she had, for she had said it only out of bitter disappointment with herself, Eodice cried, "You will not speak to me that way," and brought her hand up to slap Demetria across the face.

Demetria turned to one side, bracing for the blow, but it never came. Instead, Eodice embraced her.

"My child!" she said, and burst into tears. "By Demeter! I will not let you out of my sight until you are safely on the boat to Massalia."

::XIII::

Dawn was still hours away when Lucius tried the door to the king's palace.

The guards appointed had been silenced: *milites quieto longo affecti-- may the soldiers be affected with a long rest*, and now it was time to unbar the door.

Ianua aperta-- may the door be opened, and the bar moved on its own. An oil lamp burned to the side where the janitor-- the slave appointed at the door-- slept peacefully. With any luck, no one would know he had been there.

Lucius made his way down the empty corridor, feeling his way, not creating light because he did not trust that someone might come out of some room unexpectedly.

He went by the dining room where they had eaten that day,

and followed the corridor that led to the stairway into the tombs. That door was locked with a key, which Lucius summoned and used. He then told it to go back to its original place.

So far, an easy task. Lucius' training served him well. He thought of grammars quickly, and perfected them the first time-- except for the grammar against Demetria. He had been thoughtless and impatient. Stopping Demetria talking didn't mean Marcus would come back. In fact, the grammar might have closed her heart against him forever.

Now he was alone. He had to find the *baculum*, to augment his power and make himself irresistible. He thought for a spiteful moment that that would be better-- to become as near a god as possible, so it would not matter whether Demetria agreed or disagreed. How tiresome it was to have to guess at others' thoughts and feelings!

But he regretted the thought almost immediately upon having it.

In the storeroom, Lucius repeated what he had seen the king do, and the floor opened as it had. The chill that washed over Lucius' face when the door opened made him stand up straight. A prayer on his lips to his genius, he descended.

When he got to the bottom of the stairs, he figured it would be safe to create light, so he summoned it-- *O lucs sepulchro Etrusco-- May there be light in the Etruscan tomb--* and the scenes on the walls reappeared to him.

It was the anteroom, with the passages to the other tomb chambers, and the doors painted on three sides of the wall. His first job would be to go into those other chambers to see if doors led away from those rooms as well. King Tarquin had said that was all there was, the main room and the other two, for the Tarquins had not been kings in Rome for so long that there would be many of their ancestors buried here.

But Lucius still needed to investigate.

He approached first the room under construction, pausing at the unfinished lion-sphinxes on both sides of the door. Though their heads were still only near-shapeless blocks of stone, they made Lucius' hair on his arms stand up. Logo had said to expect anything. But what could stone do to him?

Lucius stopped, and looked over at the other opening. Here there were no lion-sphinxes, no guardians at all, it seemed. It might be better to go there first.

He was careful to keep his sandals from slapping against his feet as he walked. It was deadly silent, and he didn't want to wake anyone above. But Lucius began to feel the weight of the Etruscan spirits buried there, and it seemed as if they were beginning to whisper.

He passed the door to the earlier-made tomb room, a little chill passing the nape of his neck as he did so. The light illuminated this new room, which had a lower ceiling than the anteroom, but still tall enough to stand without stooping. Here, there was a niche, a place carved in the rock, about the size of a bed, on which a statue of a man reclining, dressed in heavy robes, had been carved.

"Tarquinius Priscus," Lucius whispered, and at the sound the statue seemed to stir or shake. It moved so little that in the uncertain light Lucius could hardly be sure it had-- until a cloud of dust rose from the king's stone head. The statue had turned its head by its neck, and now its eyes were square on Lucius.

The eyes glimmered, like those of dogs in the night, and Lucius realized that they were made of glass or some shiny stone or metal. Reflections, Lucius thought, careful to keep his tongue still and ready to perfect a grammar. He moved about the tomb chamber, his eyes on the eyes of the king's statue, and the head moved just enough, and with the tiniest of scraping sounds, to keep Lucius in its line of sight.

Whatever was causing this, it couldn't continue.

"*Cervix regis Etrusci immovens*," *The neck of the Etruscan king not moving*, Lucius whispered, tossing a grammarstone at the statue. It bounced off, and glowed on the floor. He moved again, and the statue kept its position.

Lucius sighed, and a wave of fatigue came over him, heating his face. He felt sweat on his temple, and thought of his bed at home.

"No sleep yet," he said through barely parted lips.

He looked about Priscus' chamber. It felt to him familiar,

almost homey, and this was no surprise to Lucius, for Priscus was his great-grandfather. Here the style of painting was much less elaborate than in the anteroom, and the paint was faded compared to it. It appeared the elder king had been a great lover of athletic games, for the walls contained wrestlers, runners, and acrobats. Smaller niches were marked by smaller statues, not life-sized. Painted garlands of ivy-- the crowns of victors-- decorated the walls just underneath the ceiling.

"Nothing is being protected here," Lucius thought. "I must go on to the other room, and brave those lion-sphinxes." He stooped to pick up the grammarstone, still aware of the murmuring of the spirits.

Lucius crossed the anteroom again with its six openings, three true and three false. As he looked up toward the threshold with the stairs going up, he wondered if he should turn back-- then thought of Demetria.

"I must go on," he thought. He must retrieve the *baculum*. Then perhaps she would forgive him.

He could think of no grammar against the lion-sphinxes, and it occurred to him that, unfinished, there was nothing they could do against him. Nevertheless, as he walked through the threshold he clutched the grammarstones in his pouch.

As the king said, this place was unfinished. Some of the walls were plastered, and figures beginning to emerge as painters worked on them. There was a niche where there must be a statue some day, but not yet. The floor was still broken and uneven with the cuts made into the bedrock. No one, Lucius knew in his soul, was buried here yet, and as there were no doors leading out of it, there was nowhere else to go in it.

The grammarstone light was fading, so Lucius made

another grammar to renew it, and as the room brightened, so Lucius' mood darkened. No new doors, no staircases, no indications at all that this place was anything other than it was: the home of the dead of the kings of Rome.

He stood in the center of the anteroom and sighed. He had no idea how much time had gone by, but if he didn't find the door soon, he would have to make his way back home and think of another plan. He pivoted slowly on his heel, taking in the scenes that had been painted: the heavy door with the metal nails, and the *apatanasar*; the door with the seahorses and gods; the one with the hunt.

Up above him, the sound of metal on metal. A scraping and a turning, and the song of pain that metal makes when it needs oil.

The key to the door up the staircase.

Then there was the urgent patter of sandals on stairs.

Who had found him out? He had closed the door behind him, and locked it. If the guards had been found asleep, would they immediately think to look in the tombs for an intruder?

If it were guards, Lucius could defeat them. But--

The statue. The eyes. That looked like mirrors. Mirrors that take in what is seen in a room.

Haruspices would be much more difficult.

A figure appeared on the stairs. In the light of the grammarstone, a mirror flashed at the man's side.

Words came out of Lucius' mouth: *ianua ostendens viam baculi aperta. The door showing the way of the baculum, opened.*

All three painted doors vanished, and in their place there were thresholds to darkness.

"No!" cried the *haruspex* whom Lucius recognized as

Repsuna. He brought his mirror up to Lucius' line of sight.

There was no time to think. Lucius turned away from the mirror and flung himself through the closest threshold-- the one next to the water scene-- directly opposite Repsuna. As he leapt, a knife flew just to the left of his ear.

And he found he couldn't breathe.

::XIV::

Demetria woke with the smell of fire in her nostrils.

She sat up in bed with a start, thinking at first that the house must be burning. The memory of the night before, the prodigy, the death of Marcus, the grammar of silence, everything, came flooding back, like a dream well-remembered.

But it was quiet in the women's quarters, the quiet of mid-morning, broken only by the chirp of birds rejoicing in the spring. By this time all the females of the household had been working for hours, spinning wool in the courtyard or tending to the baking in the outdoor oven or cooking in the hearth room.

"Phane!" Demetria called, but not loud enough for her aunt to hear. She thought of the fire in the courtyard, the fire in the sky, the fire where the presentation dinner had been cooked. The smell of ash and charcoal was in her hair, and on the fleeces piled on her.

They let me sleep, she thought. *I am no longer a girl, a wool-worker in my mother's company. I am almost a guest in my father's house. I am waiting to be carried off to Massalia.*

I am a bride-to-be.

She got up, threw a dress over her, brushed her hair out, put a band in it to hold it back. Hungry, she made her way to the hearth room, which was quiet except for the hiss of the fire and the bubbling of barley porridge in a pot next to it. Two slaves, one with a stirring spoon, stood up when she arrived, as if they'd been instructed to wait for her.

"Mistress," said one of them, "a visitor for you."

"A visitor? Who is it?"

"A Roman," said the other. "He sits just outside the courtyard."

"Has he been waiting long?"

"We will get him," said the first.

Gnaeus appeared in the doorway of the hearth room, like a spirit from a long-ago dream.

"Gnaeus!" she cried, and went to embrace him. "Old friend! You are welcome." Her heart soared to see the kind-hearted young man who reminded him of adventures already lived and therefore more sweetly remembered.

"You are better guarded than the priestess of Vesta," he said, smiling as he pulled back and held her hand. "I could only persuade them to let me see you when I said I was on an errand from the shrine of Numa Pompilius."

Demetria glanced at the slaves who stood by the threshold. "It seems I am the property of another, by Hercules," she said with a sigh. She still couldn't bring herself to say *By Hera*.

He nodded. "Perhaps, then, you have not yet heard the news."

"What news?"

"That Marcus Junius Brutus is dead."

Demetria put her hands to her face, fresh tears coming. "I knew," she whispered. "I saw."

Gnaeus cocked his head. "Then you know also of the great prodigy on the Capitoline Hill, and that the Shield has gone?"

"Yes, that too."

"The elders met together this morning with the king, who asked the *haruspices* the meaning of the prodigy and of the disappearance of the Shield." He put his hand on Demetria's shoulder. "*It is the goddess of Death, Vanth, who has taken the Shield,* they said. It is a powerful message from the gods of Etruria. The Shield is no longer to be held by the Romans, but has been transferred to the Etruscans. So long as they hold it in their power, Rome shall remain Etruscan, and the Romans shall be their servants."

Demetria sniffed, held back a sob. "There was no news that the Shield had been summoned back by ancient lore?"

"No, dear one," said Gnaeus. "That would be something, if it were true. No. The seers insist that Vanth now possesses the Shield and will keep it safe."

Demetria wiped her tears with her hands, and a slave rushed to give her a linen cloth. Maybe she should run to the middle of Rome, she thought, call the whole town to her, and say that the *haruspices* were lying! But there were several problems with that approach: no one would believe her, there was nothing they could do about it, and there was no way she could get out of the house.

"Where is Nauarchus?" she cried suddenly to the slaves. Maybe he could help her. She didn't know how, but it didn't matter. Even just to talk to him might help.

"In Ostia, mistress," said one of the slaves. "This very morning he has gone back to his ship in Ostia to oversee repairs."

"And when shall he return?"

"Not for several days, mistress."

Demetria slumped down on a stool, fingering the tear-stained cloth. She gazed at the embers of the hearth fire. The fire filled her eyes with the colors of sunset, the colors of death.

"The funeral for Marcus is today," said Gnaeus. "I must be off soon to join it."

"Yes, Gnaeus. Thank you for coming."

"But there is one more piece of news. About Lucius."

Demetria continued to stare at the fire, said nothing.

Gnaeus sat close to Demetria and whispered in her ear, "He asked me to tell you. He has gone searching for the second *baculum*-- in the Etruscan Land of the Dead."

Demetria looked up at the slaves, who seemed not to be trying to overhear Gnaeus' secret. They did not speak Latin well, but you seldom knew the truth with slaves.

"He went without me," she whispered back.

"He seemed to think you--"

"Yes," said Demetria, louder, and hit the air with her fist. "He thought. He is always thinking."

"And one other thing, my mistress," said Gnaeus. "Before he left, he asked me to give you these."

Gnaeus brought a small pouch from the fold of his cloak. He extended it to Demetria, and when she took it into the palm of her hand, she could feel the vibrations of grammarstones on her skin.

"No!" Demetria whispered. "He can't have." She looked inside, and emptied the stones onto her other hand. "I can't believe it," she said. "He needs these. He needs all of these."

"But you must now see to the Shield, my Demetria."

"He cannot think that I know how to--" She stopped, thought for a moment, then recast her words. "Gnaeus. Will you be going back to Logo now?"

"I expect. There is nothing for me to do here, and if the *haruspices* capture me, they will make me lead them to the shrine. What a frightful fire they will make if they succeed in doing that. The Shield gone, the Shrine burned... and if Lucius does not come back with the *baculum*..."

Demetria balled a fist and shook it as she spoke. "But that won't happen. It can't. It won't. You're right-- you must go back to Logo. But then you must come back to me."

"What? How?"

Demetria fingered the grammarstones in the pouch, calculating. Lucius had left her seven. But for the grammar needed to summon the Shield, maybe she would only need one. "My Gnaeus, I want you to go to Logo and ask him for a grammar."

"A grammar? The words--?"

"Yes, the exact words of the grammar that brings the Shield to the summoner."

"There is such a thing?"

"If there is, Logo will know it. Now, to--"

At that moment, Eodice entered the room with other slaves carrying the day's shopping, and Demetria had only the briefest instant to hide the pouch in the fold of her dress.

Eodice's attention was not on Demetria, but on the slaves

at the threshold. "Who is this visitor?" she barked. "Who allowed him in to see my daughter?"

"Phane, mistress," they said together, and then one said, "He gave--"

Eodice turned back to Gnaeus and spoke gently, in Latin. "I am sorry, sir, my daughter is to be married and she cannot be seen with other men."

Gnaeus stood up and bowed deeply. "My lady," he said. "I am not other men. I am a messenger from the shrine of Numa Pompilius. On a sacred duty, by Egeria."

Demetria held back a smile. Gnaeus was not clever, but yet, he was in a way, too.

"May all the gods bless us," said Eodice, and bowed herself. "Then I trust you have delivered your message, sir?"

Gnaeus bowed again. "Yes, my lady. I shall be making my way back now, lady." And with a bow to Demetria, he departed.

"Phane!" Eodice cried, turning her head outside the threshold. "Phane, I would speak with you!" And she left for the courtyard.

Demetria gave a look at the slaves, and an especially hard one at the one who had almost given away the gift of the stones. Then she fled back to the woman's quarters, and once there, recounted the stones and rolled them on her fingers before hiding them safely so that it did not matter whether the slaves told.

She put her hand to her nose, remembering the sour smell of exploded grammarstones, remembering all that Lucius had done with the *baculum* and the stones to get them back from the mirror world where, months ago, they had journeyed together.

The Shield of Numa! Demetria thought, hefting the bag again as she dropped it into its hiding place, a hole carved out of a soft spot in the mortar of the floor, and covered with a rug. *Lucius will retrieve the* baculum, *and I the Shield. I guess we are still together-- in saving Rome.*

Demetria spent the rest of the day in the women's quarters praying to the gods that the *haruspices* would not try to destroy the shield as they had the *baculum*, and that Logo would understand Gnaeus' request and that he would come back soon with the grammar.

Meanwhile, the funeral procession of Marcus Junius Brutus went through the Greek quarter, and Demetria was allowed to watch it from the gate to the courtyard, no nearer. It took the opposite route that the priests had taken the day before, ending where they had began. As the women of the Junius family wailed and walked, Demetria shed her own tears quietly.

That evening, after the procession, Demetria had another visitor, one neither Eodice nor Istocles could deny.

"Come to the hearth room," said one of the slaves. "The prince of Rome."

Arruns requested that the room be cleared, and Istocles, his eyes wide at the visit of Tarquin's son, ordered it.

"I am surprised to see you, Arruns," said Demetria as they were seated next to the fire. "I was the one who was always chasing after you."

Arruns coughed. "My father sent me. He wants to know if you know where Lucius is. The two sons of his sister, gone. It is not well with the family."

He was so pale and sickly, it was a wonder he could walk at

all, thought Demetria. "Why does King Tarquin want to know where Lucius is? Now that his brother is dead, does he want Lucius dead also?"

"My father does not wish the Junius family ill."

"But perhaps it was lucky for him a rival was killed."

"He did not order Marcus' death. Marcus was the Salian priest who was holding the shield of Numa. He went into the grove next to the temple. When he came out, he no longer had the shield or his life."

"Then it must have been the goddess Vanth," Demetria concluded scornfully. "If she uses a throwing dagger to murder Romans."

"You know the weapon that was used?" Arruns said.

"Doesn't everyone?" The memory of the dagger in Marcus' back chilled her. Had not the dagger been found there, and the manner of his death related to all?

Or had she spoken too much?

"No, I don't think so, though I am not surprised you do!" Arruns shot her a look that was half jealousy, half admiration. "My father is worried. Someone broke into our palace last night. The front door was unbarred and the guards sleeping at their posts. Our janitor was sleeping as always. But no one was found inside the house, and nothing was taken. The *haruspices* took the omens and said that a spirit had come to visit my grandmother. She was asked what she had dreamt that night and she said she believed she had seen the spirit of Marcus."

"And how does Lucius come into this?"

"Someone came to the palace last night. Lucius is gone this morning. The *haruspices* speak of spirits. We do not know what to believe."

Demetria thought of her last conversation with Lucius. He had not told her where to find the entrance to the Etruscan Land of the Dead. But she could guess. "So the seers of Etruria do not know where Lucius is?"

"Or they will not say. At times they become very mysterious."

Demetria gazed at the fire for a moment. Why would the *haruspices* not tell Tarquin where Lucius was? Unless they wanted to dispose of him themselves, without having to explain anything to the king. "I do not know where he is," she said finally.

Arruns coughed again, doubled over, and when he looked up, a trickle of sweat had gone down his temple. Though he looked a boy still, what came from his mouth was deadly serious. "I think you do. We have not known each other these past years for nothing, Demetria. We are all growing into men and women. You will be married, I hear. And I will be king someday, if my father keeps power. At that time, I will be able to help your father and your family. I will also be able to help Lucius and the house of Junius. If he come back into his right mind, he could be a partner with me."

Demetria hesitated, and she knew as she did so that Arruns had guessed the truth. "I still don't know," she said, "why you want him. He is harmless, a simpleton."

"Don't protect him, Demetria," he said. "You may think he is safe, but our enemies will find him."

"Our enemies?"

"The *haruspices* have informed my father. There are families in Rome that want the Etruscans to leave Rome, who have never accepted us or our ways. Of course it is power they are after. They have heard the prophecies about Rome-- and even without them, it is easy to see that we can be greater than other Etruscan cities. The gods are with us. Who says these people were not the ones who killed Marcus, to make Romans suspicious of us?"

"The *haruspices* have their own purposes, and none of them are friends of Rome."

"You are Greek. You know nothing of their work."

Demetria thought hard. How much to tell Arruns? How much did he really know? He always was able to speak well. He had tutors, he studied and practiced the art of speaking. But what was in his heart? Was he a true friend of Lucius?

"If I help you," Demetria said, "the king must tell my father that I have leave to travel freely-- to search for Lucius. I do not know where he is. But I might know the road he took."

"Road?"

"I can tell you no more until the king frees me from this house."

"All right," said Arruns. "I will take the message to my father. He has power over all residents of this city, Greek, Roman, or Etruscan."

As Arruns summoned his escort, Demetria sighed. She hoped that Arruns was telling the truth, but in any case, she needed her freedom to search for the Shield. Gnaeus might return with the Shield-summoning grammar in a couple of days-- or never. She had to do what she could on her own, whether Gnaeus, or Lucius, for that matter, came back.

And what of Nauarchus? He would return soon from Ostia after the repairs to his ship were completed.

May that time go slowly, thought Demetria. *Very slowly.*

::XV::

Lucius was underwater.

One moment he was jumping through a portal with a yell, the next there was salt water in his mouth, and all around him. He never felt a splash-- he was just in it.

It was dark, so dark it must be night wherever this water was, or else underground. Lucius immediately thought of the time, almost a year before, when he was drowning in the Tiber River. He was trying to swim it, and the current had taken him under. At that time, he had only a few moments to call out to whatever gods were listening, and something or someone had brought him to the surface of the water.

Could he float to the surface? The pressure on his ears told him he must be very deep, and there was always the possibility that he was in some kind of underground sea that did not have a surface.

Lucius waved his arm in front of him, groping for his bag

of grammarstones. Once his hand was on them, he tried to open his mouth to perfect a grammar, but the first word-- *aqua-- water--* came out sounding nothing like it.

He would not be able to speak a grammar here.

For the first time, Lucius was afraid. He had been able to hold his breath thus far, for it seemed that as he went through the threshold he must have breathed in deeply and held it. But now, not knowing what to do, his spirit was telling him to let go-- breathe the precious bubbles of air still in his lungs, and take a new breath.

But there was no air to breathe.

He coughed, and a big burst of air thrust out from his mouth. Stars began to pop before his eyes.

"No," he thought. "I've survived drowning once. I can do it again."

He was still clutching the stones in his pouch, but they were useless. Unless--

He closed his fist around a grammarstone, and brought it slowly up, the water pushing against his hand. More breath came out as he opened his mouth. There was almost nothing left in his lungs, which were starting to ache.

He put the grammarstone in his mouth, slipped it between his lips, and held it behind his teeth. And then he whispered, trying to open his mouth as little as possible:

"*O spiritus ore et nari magi magistri.*" *May there be breath in the nose and lungs of the master mage.*

Immediately he could breathe! The nearness of the grammarstone must have helped the sound leave his mouth in words.

Lucius held the grammarstone between his cheek and gum,

vibrating with the power of the grammar Lucius had created. He breathed in deeply, and exhaled through his nostrils. Bubbles tickled his upper lip and passed away.

"By Hercules! Thank the gods! Thank Egeria!" Lucius thought, careful not to open his mouth to the stinging salt water. He took another grammarstone from the pouch and held it in his hand, making another whispered grammar for light.

His voice came out in a hiss of bubbles. The grammarstone glowed brightly as he held it in his fingertips, and for the first time, he was able to see where he was.

He was standing on a sandy seafloor. Small fish darted back and forth in and out of the light. Seaweed waved. It was truly the final home of those who died in storms.

Testing his ability to breathe, Lucius pushed against the water with his arms and felt with his sandals. Sand plumed up around his feet as he walked, and he understood why he wasn't floating to the surface: the grammarstones were weighing him down, like an anchor. If he let go the grammarstones, he was quite likely to rise immediately to the surface of the water.

But he dismissed that thought as quickly as it came up.

Before long he came to a set of rocks protruding from the sand. A few more paces further, more rocks appeared on the first rocks' left and right. He was near shore, or perhaps a reef. He needed to find a way out of the water, for it was clear this was not the Etruscan Land of the Dead. Logo had said nothing about ocean depths.

But almost as soon as he found the rocks, Lucius found something else: wooden beams all in a row, and held together by a long wooden spine.

"A ship!" Lucius thought. "A ship that was lost on these rocks. The spirits of men fled from this place. So perhaps there is a door to the Land of the Dead."

Lucius made his way through the shattered remains of the ship. Metals winked in the sand-- knives, nails, even coins-- and broken pieces of painted pottery as well. Lucius picked up a large shard, which had once been part of a *krater*, a wine bowl, and could make out the face of Dionysus, Greek god of wine. Amphoras, large storage jars, were piled and strewn everywhere, showing that this was a merchant ship once, with a cargo of perfumed oil, possibly even someone that Demetria's family had known.

Then, there it was, as Lucius knew it must be: the white skull of a drowned sailor, his flesh picked clean by action of water and fish looking for food. As Lucius explored on, he found another, and another, some attached to bodies that still had the remnants of tunics and cloaks clinging to their torsos.

Suddenly, Lucius was freezing cold. He tried to make a sign to ward off the evil eye, but before he had finished he heard something in the center of his brain, the first sound he had heard since coming to this watery land of the dead.

"Phane!"

It was an urgent whisper, but sad, as if whoever had spoken it had lost hope.

At first, Lucius thought the sound made no sense, but even as it came again-- "Phane!" -- he realized it was the name of Demetria's aunt, a woman as close to her as Gallia had been.

Lucius spoke another grammar: "*Spiritus loquens apparens*," *May the spirit speaking be visible*.

An outline of a man formed in front of Lucius. The

grammarstone light shone through it, but as it formed, the spirit also darkened, and it finally became that of a young man with a short beard, who had once been squat, sturdy, and long-armed.

"Phane!" The mouth of the spirit moved, but the sound, again, seemed to come forth in the center of Lucius' head.

"Spirit," Lucius said, in Latin, with the help of the grammarstone still on the side of his cheek. "Why do you call for Phane? Do you know Demetria, Greek girl of Rome?"

The spirit groaned, and it chilled Lucius even more than hearing the name the first time. His neck began to hurt, and he knew he must get out of this water soon. The grammarstones helped to keep him warm, but only so much.

Again the spirit groaned, and Lucius was about to speak again, but it finally said, "Phane, my wife and my child."

"Aristoxenus!" Lucius said. "You are the husband of Phane!"

The spirit nodded, and lowered its head in deep sorrow.

"Why are you still here?" Lucius asked. There had been a ceremony in Ostia, on the beach, for the poor man and his crew, and Aristoxenus' father had asked the gods for his safe trip to the Underworld, where Hades ruled and all Greeks went to join their ancestors in death.

"I do not go," said Aristoxenus. "I do not go. Not yet. Phane!"

"Phane cannot come to you, nor you to Phane!" Lucius said. "You have died. You are a spirit. You must join your family and have your rest."

"Tell Phane! Please. Please tell her. Then I go."

"You want me to give Phane a message?"

The spirit nodded vigorously. "Tell her."

"I will take the message, Aristoxenus. But can you tell me, in return? Can you help me?"

The spirit did not move, but cocked its head, as if waiting for Lucius to continue.

"Do you know the way to the Etruscan Land of the Dead from here? Do you know a way out from here, a door, an opening, a cave, where an Etruscan would go?"

Aristoxenus said, "Tell her."

"Yes, I will," said Lucius.

"Tell her: *eis archonta nauos gemasthai exestin.*"

It was in Greek, and after Aristoxenus repeated it a couple of times, he realized what it said, for he had had Greek lessons: *it is permitted to marry the captain of the ship.*

It is permitted to marry the captain of the ship! Lucius thought. *To whom is it permitted? To Phane?*

"Tell her: *eis archonta nauos gemasthai exestin.*"

Lucius bowed. "It will be done," he said.

Aristoxenus nodded, waved his hand, and closed it, as if beckoning someone to come. Then he disappeared.

For a moment, there was nothing, no sound, just the pain on the back of Lucius neck that was getting stronger, the chill in his limbs, and the grammarstone light, that was fading ever so slightly.

But then there was a lot more than nothing.

From all sides there came a rushing, a disturbance of waters, and soon Lucius was surrounded: a half dozen or more huge beasts were circling him.

"Hippocamps!" Lucius cried.

They were seahorses, creatures as large as terrestrial horses, with the heads of horses and the bodies of fish. They had tails and fins that allowed them to swim like the wind, and their scales were spangled, in colors of silver, light blue, and gold. Their manes were of seaweed, and their eyes were gem-red.

"Aristoxenus, help!" Lucius cried through the water. "What is this in return for my favor to you?"

But the spirit did not come, and the seahorses continued to circle Lucius, buffeting him with the heavy beating of their fins and tails. They even seemed to be closing the circle, and it was only the grammarstones that were keeping Lucius anchored to the seafloor. As they whirled about, he also turned, and more than once lost his footing and his legs flew out from under him.

Kneeling, Lucius clutched his grammarstones again, his eyes full of the twinkling, coruscating light reflected from the hippocamps' scales. What could he do? He thought first of creating spears and thrusting them between the eyes of the twelve creatures. But they were beautiful, and he didn't want to kill them. Besides, were they trying to kill him? They were only stopping him from moving forward.

But then the circle got noticeably smaller, and the buffeting worse. Now and then, a tail would pass in front of Lucius' face, and once, a sharp end cut through his cloak and tunic on the outside of his shoulder.

"Must I kill them?" Lucius thought. "Or will they kill me first?"

A passing hippocamp lowered its neck, and quick as a flash, nipped at his arm, drawing blood.

Lucius thought of spears, and part of a grammar came from his mouth, but at the last minute, he thought of something else. He took a grammarstone from his pouch, and when a hippocamp came near, he held the stone up to it. The creature thrust its neck. Lucius' hand came away stinging. He'd been bit.

But the horse had taken the grammarstone.

"*Equus maris domitus!*" *May the horse of the sea be tamed.*

The hippocamps fell back, and ceased their circling. Instead, they swished their tails and lowered their necks, their shining eyes all on Lucius. He shook his hand. The salt water made the bite sting the worse, and then there was the nip on his shoulder as well.

The horse that had swallowed the grammarstone did not swish its tail or retreat from Lucius. It became as still as a seahorse could, and watched its new master.

"*O frenum habenad ori equi maris,*" Lucius said. *I summon a bit and a rein on the mouth of the seahorse.*

Immediately there appeared a halter of gold around the seahorse's head. Lucius swam over to the beast and took one side of the rein. Bracing one leg against the scaled flank of the horse, he swung his other over its back. He took the other side of the rein, and pulled. The bit dug into the hippocamp's mouth, and it snorted and tossed its head.

"*Equus maris viam baculi inveniens,*" he said into the ear of the horse-- *may the horse of the sea be finding the way of the staff--* and it jerked forward, almost throwing Lucius off his back. But Lucius clamped his legs around the fish body, and took a hank of the seaweed mane. It was slippery, but he could hold it.

The hippocamp swam forward faster than any horse Lucius had ever ridden. He wished he had also summoned a saddle. And he wished that the door to the Etruscan Land of the Dead would be close, because he didn't think he had the strength to hold on for long. But now there was no getting to the pouch of grammarstones, not without losing hold of the mane and the horse itself.

Lucius simply had to trust that the grammar he'd made was correct.

::XVI::

The hippocamp soon left the bottom of the sea and took Lucius upwards. The grammarstone light now illuminated nothing except Lucius, the horse, and whatever fish that strayed nearby.

Gradually, they ascended, and gradually the ache on Lucius' ears grew less. Finally, they came to rocks, and an opening in the rocks, which turned into a tunnel of a sort.

The tunnel opened up into what must have been a cavern, for soon the sea horse found another tunnel which closed about them even tighter than the first. Then they entered a second cavern, then a third tunnel, and when they came to the next cavern, the horse swam swiftly up, so that Lucius had trouble holding on. But then its head broke the surface of the water, and thrust its body up so that Lucius also broke the surface.

For the first time since he had gone through the portal, Lucius breathed without the help of a grammarstone.

He slipped off the horse, clutched a rock in the middle of

the pool where the horse had brought him, made light on another grammarstone and threw it away from him. The stone clattered on the edge of the pool and illuminated a cavern about twice as tall as he was, rocky, but otherwise featureless.

The seahorse swam below him, its eyes on Lucius, tail now and then splashing and troubling the otherwise quiet pool. Lucius wondered how long the taming grammar would last, and if he could use the horse to go somewhere else if there was no portal here. The hippocamp seemed completely placid and in his power.

But to find a portal, Lucius needed to get to shore. He couldn't really swim with the grammarstones, so he dipped his toe in the water. Immediately the hippocamp raised up so that he could mount its back, and it swam him over to the shore, flicking its long body to help him off and onto the pebbly edge.

Lucius now felt colder than ever, because at least he had gotten used to the water temperature. Now he was wet, his cloak was dripping and hanging heavily about him, and the air inside the cave was quite cold. He made a grammar to dry himself-- *may the water on the skin and clothes of the master mage be gone (aqua dermati et vetibus magistri magi disappartu)*-- and gradually he dried, and his cloak felt lighter and lighter. Finally he was able to wrap his cloak tightly about him and feel a kind of warmth.

The hippocamp still lay just under the surface of the water, and Lucius considered making a grammar to make it stay, but thought better of it when he put his hand into the still wet bag (he hadn't included that in what should dry) and realized he had used quite a few grammarstones already, and he didn't even know if he was in the Etruscan Land of the Dead. After all, wasn't Aristoxenus Greek, and wouldn't he show the way to the Greek Land of the Dead? But he had made a grammar for the hippocamp-- find a way to the *baculum*. And seahorse probably knew a lot more than they let on, especially since they didn't speak.

In any case, there was nothing to do but try to find a way out of the cave, and, if possible, without using a grammarstone. He sat down on a rock and carefully counted, finding twenty-eight left. Even just making light in a cavern would take a lot of these. He would have to be very careful.

He replaced the stones in the bag, once more drew his cloak about him, and picked his way over rocks to the walls of the cavern. His journey took him in a rough circle around the pool, and toward the end of it, he found an opening in the rock, and something like stairs going up. What's more, someone had carved into the rock on the left-hand side of the opening what Lucius knew were Etruscan letters. He knew more Etruscan than Greek, so when he read the inscription,

CA PERA VANTHIAS

he knew immediately where he was: the house of Vanth.

"Beware, Vanth is here!" Lucius whispered, and was surprised to hear the sounds echo all around the chamber.

"I didn't speak that loudly," he said, a little louder, and the echo came up stronger.

"Loud," he said firmly, and the echo was like a shout, and a pebble fell from a ledge halfway up the cave wall and fell with a clatter.

"How silly I am!" Lucius thought, and turned to go up the stairs-- it was the only way out-- but something made him stop.

It was a breath of air against his cheek.

Previously, the air had not moved at all, as Lucius would've expected in an enclosed cave. This air came from above, from the stairway, and that, Lucius thought, made sense, too. Nevertheless, it chilled him.

The pressure against his cheek continued to build, and Lucius passed the grammarstone light in front of him. "What is it?" he said aloud. "Where--"

Something flew at him; Lucius put his hands over his head as he dropped to the ground, rolled, and it roared over the top of him, with a shriek that stabbed him like a knife in the back, and then again through his chest as the echo multiplied the sound.

It wasn't wind-- it was a spirit.

It flew about the chamber, making a terrifying, echoing roar, and then came at Lucius again. All he could see was milky white tatters-- like a cloak that had been cut every which way-- and something like a face that Lucius' genius must have told him not to look at, for he shielded his eyes with his forearm as the thing slowed and settled in front of him.

The shrieking continued until Lucius knew he could take it no longer, and he screamed back at it *SILENTIUM CAVERNE-- may there be silence in the cave--* and it was silent. But Lucius knew, as sweat trickled down his hot temples, that he had stopped himself from doing any more grammar in that place, for if there was silence on the monster, then there was silence on him as well.

Lucius thought of fleeing up the stairs, but the spirit must have also, for it flew about and blocked Lucius' way. Lucius looked quickly up at it as it hovered in front of the threshold, silent and horrible. Its face was like a mask, something an actor or performer would put in front of his face, but uglier. The mask had huge eyes and mouth, and traces of blood came from all the openings. The mouth was twisted down as if to emit the most despairing groan a dead soul could create.

Dead soul! Marcus! Lucius thought. He knelt, heavy with grief. The Salian priests wore masks, too. Was this his own brother, come to haunt him?

Oh, by all the gods, let it not be!

Some god must have answered him, for in an instant, another thought in Lucius' heart, a memory of Gallia from long ago. She was telling him about a kind of spirit that put a mask in front of its face. What was its name?

"Larva!" Lucius thought to himself, and Gallia's own voice came to him.

"The larva is a spirit of one who led a life of sadness," she had said. "It has done in life many things of which it is ashamed. It is restless for it refuses to join its family in the Land of the Dead. It is too ashamed to be seen by them; it went to its death thinking it could not be forgiven."

"Why does it have a mask, dear nurse?" Lucius had asked.

"It must not show its true face. If it does, then all will know who has done these terrible things, for in death there are no secrets."

Lucius forced himself to look at the mask, terrifying though it was. As the spirit hovered there, the mask seemed to be real, to be made of wood or stone, and to be supported by the larva's breath itself. The blood may have been paint; the border around the horrible frown was carved and bowed outwards. There were nicks and bruises in it, where it must have hit against cave walls.

"If it is a real mask..." Lucius whispered, but did not finish the thought.

The thing hovered in front of the stairway, screaming silently, and Lucius buried his face behind his cloak and forearm. As he did this, a measure of courage returned to him. The spirit could not scream, and that made all the difference.

Lucius stood up, his eyes tightly shut, and forced himself to approach the larva, which floated just out of his reach, the tatters of the spirit cloak it wore bouncing like ribbons pinned to a stick. He let his own cloak fall to his ankles, and it brushed against his stomach that seemed to be five times larger than normal.

Lucius grasped a grammarstone, opened his eyes, aimed, and threw the stone at the mask. The larva dodged, just a flick of its spirit breath, and the stone went flying up to the ceiling, then clattered down the stairs where it rested just on the other side of the threshold.

"It can't do that every time," Lucius thought, his eyes shut again.

He threw another stone, drawing, aiming, and throwing as fast as he could. The larva dodged again. The stone came down crazily, bounced away, and into the dark beyond where Lucius had made light.

Lucius scolded himself-- another grammarstone lost.

"One more," he thought, and his hand went into the bag. This time when Lucius looked, the spirit's mask seemed to grin for a second, as if to say, *go ahead, try it.*

Lucius stopped in mid-throw. Instead, he opened his eyes, looked into those of the mask, and breathed.

It was not cold enough that his breath was visible, but he felt it leave his lips, tickle them, and knew it was hanging in the air between him and the larva. It was warm.

Lucius breathed out again; he could feel the fear in his belly contracting it, and he coughed. The larva came closer.

One more breath. The larva could not resist the warmth of it, its cold spirit next to Lucius' warmth. It came close, as if to suck in the breath through the gaping mouth of the mask.

Lucius cupped his hands to his mouth and blew. The spirit shook and fell back in its wake, but then rushed forward.

That was when Lucius' hands flashed out from his mouth where he had cupped them, and took hold of the mask. He wrenched it away-- it came easily away from the icy shards of spirit that held it to the tatters of the larva-- turned, and cast it as far as he could.

The mask might have splashed in the pool, or against the far wall of the cave. It was dark, and there was no sound in the cavern. But when Lucius turned around, he saw a spirit face so frightened and anguished that he knew no longer would he have to worry about its screams.

The larva fled.

Lucius was alone in the cave. He stepped over the threshold, and his sandal scraped on the grit covering the stone stair step. He stamped his foot, rattled the grammarstones in their bag. All of these things made their proper sounds.

Lucius knelt down and emptied the contents of his stomach onto the wall of the passage, retching over and over until there was nothing left. He would never forget that mask or that frightened face that the mask had covered.

What else must be here? he thought. He was careful to say

nothing aloud, for fear that another larva would come, or worse. He still had the grammarstones, but he knew he would have to be even more careful now. "Never make silence," he thought. "Leave space for the grammar to work."

Lucius collected the grammarstone that had fallen on the threshold, and decided not to look for the one that had bounced away. Time, he thought, was more important than one grammarstone, and any grammar he spoke to bring the stone back would have to be aloud.

The Master Mage of Rome stood up, steadied himself, wiped his face, and made his way up the staircase.

::XVII::

"Demetria, wake, the king has need of you."

It was early the next day, after Arruns had visited, and the second since Lucius had disappeared. The sun had not yet risen, and would have been hidden in gloom if it had. Late rains had come, maybe the last of the rainy season.

Phane was the one who roused Demetria from her bed. Demetria threw on a dress, sandals, and cloak, and Phane combed her hair and placed her headband. While Phane was combing, Demetria woke up enough to think of the pouch of grammarstones Lucius had given her. She affixed it to a leather shoulder strap and had it at her side as they went out to meet the king's guard waiting in the hearth room.

The two soldiers, armed with shortswords, hustled her away without letting Eodice hand Demetria a bowl of porridge.

They tracked through mud and around puddles. Even where the street was well-paved, the rain made the going slick, and more than once Demetria slipped trying to keep up with the guards' pace.

"So fast and so early!" Demetria told the guards. "What is so important on this rainy day?"

One guard eyed her, and the other told her to stay quiet.

It began to rain heavier just as they turned into the Pavement of Audience, and though they ran, they were nearly wet through when they came to the front door of the palace. The guards on duty opened the doors for them, and for a moment, before her eyes accustomed themselves to the dim light on the inside, Demetria could see nothing. But then there was the hole in the ceiling with rain coming down from it and into the pool, and on the other side, a guard holding Gnaeus by the arm.

"Gnaeus!" Demetria cried.

He shook his head, and fell in step with the guards as they walked out of the entrance hall and toward the back of the palace. They stopped only when they had reached a room with chairs ranged against the wall and lamp stands with candles burning, making a thin haze of gray, sweet-smelling smoke.

Despite the chairs, no one was sitting. The king was there with the three *haruspices*, Turanquil, Velthur, and Repsuna; Arruns stood to the side, his expression unreadable. He shook his head slightly when she glanced over. Was he saying, "You are in trouble" or "Don't say anything" or "I failed"? Maybe all three.

The guards stood in the wide threshold of the audience room, Gnaeus and Demetria in the middle, and the Etruscans against the far wall. Turanquil was the first to speak, in a kinder voice than Demetria had anticipated.

"We regret your walk was wet," she said. "Someone get the girl a dry cloak."

"No," said Demetria, realizing that without a cloak they would see and might ask about the pouch of grammarstones.

"It will take a moment, then you will be warm," said the king. A slave pulled off her cloak and left with it.

"The pouch," Turanquil said.

Another slave waited as Demetria took it from her shoulder. Turanquil looked inside, looked back at Demetria, then kept it.

Demetria balled her fists but said nothing. *What a fool I was*, she thought. *But I was half-awake! No one should be brought to a king so early.*

Turanquil nodded at the king, and he stepped forward. "Demetria, daughter of Istocles. My son Arruns tells me you are the closest friend that Lucius Junius called Brutus ever had."

"Arruns was a friend as well," Demetria said softly. She tried to catch his eye, but he was deliberately looking down. He scraped a sandal on the polished floor, and coughed.

"Brutus is in danger," said Turanquil. "There are those who want him dead."

Demetria said nothing. She was not scared; there had been almost no time to be scared yet, what with all her half-awake dodging of puddles. But Arruns' silence made her uneasy.

"Arruns says you know where he is," the king went on. "Please tell us."

Both Turanquil and the king were speaking in what sounded like soft, kind voices.

"I told Arruns-- he could have told you-- I don't know the answer to this question."

"What was this man doing?" said Velthur sharply.

Demetria jumped. She was truly awake now.

Velthur was pointing to Gnaeus. "He visited you yesterday, and we caught him leaving Rome under cover of night on the road to the shrine of Numa."

"He was going back to his home, Portentia."

"With a message from you or from Brutus?"

"Brutus knows no one in Portentia."

Turanquil said, "It would be far better if you told the truth."

"Wise seer, I think it is you who must know where he is," said Demetria. She knew she spoke too boldly. If they had been alone, Turanquil would have struck her.

As if reading her thoughts, Turanquil said, "I must speak alone with this one." She fished in a fold of her robe, and brought out a mirror.

"No!" Demetria said, now truly afraid. "King, my master. If you want me to tell you anything about Lucius, she must not be allowed to hurt me-- or poor Gnaeus here."

"No one is going to hurt you," Turanquil said quickly, but the king put up his hand.

"No mirrors," he said.

Turanquil put hers away, scowling.

"Young woman, I understand you are to be married."

"Yes, king," Demetria whispered.

"He is a good man?"

"Yes."

"It is well. And you do not want to marry Brutus?"

Demetria hesitated.

"Is it your wish to be married to a simpleton rather than to a wealthy man of your own people?"

"If Brutus-- Lucius-- returns..."

"But if he remains a simpleton?"

Demetria thought of how Lucius had made the grammar against her. She was still angry at him, angrier than she had ever been. But her heart was not all for Nauarchus.

"No one," she said, eyes down, "wishes to marry a man without a mind."

Arruns broke his silence, harshly: "Why would you protect a person you do not want to marry, and who may be in danger because he cannot think for himself?"

She turned to him. "I am not protecting him, prince. I do not know where he is." *Arruns!* Demetria thought. *Why is he so angry? I told him I needed to be free to discover where Lucius has gone.*

Tarquin said, "Enough. Peace, my son. You have done what I willed. Take them away. We will speak with her again."

"But don't let them use the mirror against me," Demetria said as she was being turned by two guards with hands on her arms. "You will lose me; I can never help you then."

The king did not answer.

The guards hustled her and Gnaeus away, separating them immediately. She was put in a bedroom with a small, shuttered window that let in a patch of gloomy light when opened. There was a bed here with a mattress and a fleece covering it. The shutter opened onto a wooded area that slanted down with the slope of the hill. But there was no getting out of the window-- it was much too small. The door, of course, was guarded.

"So much for moving freely about," Demetria thought to herself. She wondered where they had taken Gnaeus, whether she would get a chance to speak to him again. She hoped he could somehow keep the location of the Shrine a secret, but the *haruspices* were very persuasive with their mirrors.

May some god allow him to escape, she prayed.

And could she get free somehow? She paced the room, touching the rough brick walls, opening and closing the shutter, but finally, as the initial burst of anxiety and fear faded, she sat down on the bed, sighed, and began to think again of how she had been woken so early.

The door swung open and Turanquil appeared carrying a lit lamp. In her other hand was the pouch of grammarstones. She stepped aside to let a guard bring in a chair.

"Leave us," she said to the guard, and he shut the door behind her.

"Give me back what is mine," Demetria said, as Turanquil sat and adjusted her skirts.

Turanquil smiled, and leaned forward with the bag. "If you wish to play at Roman mage, you may do so," she said. She was not wearing her headdress, and with her long hair coiled and pinned behind her, almost looked like a grandmother. "Though you think you can hurt us with these stones, I have no intention of hurting you."

Demetria took the bag and took her time rethreading the strap through the pouch and adjusting it on her shoulder.

Turanquil watched her, a half-smile on her face, and waited till she was done before she spoke. "Now then. I have restored what is yours. We will speak, lady to lady."

Demetria said nothing, but thought of how strange it would be to have Turanquil as a grandmother. Did *haruspices* have husbands?

Turanquil sat back in her chair. "As you say, of course we know where Lucius is. We also know why he is there."

"We."

"*Haruspices*. The king does not."

"So why did you bring me to him and act as if--?"

"Some things it is better the king not know. We needed to bring you here to talk. Things that must be said between you and me alone."

"I don't--"

"We want you to go after him."

Demetria's mouth dropped open. "Go. After him?"

"We could go. Doubtless. And it would be a friendly place for us to be, though cold and dark. But he would not come back with us. He would attack us, and possibly defeat us."

"Why don't you just wait for him to come back?"

"He will die, and we don't want him dead."

"How do you know?"

She ignored the question. "Marcus Junius the Younger is dead, as you know. The Junius family now has only one son. If the last son dies, there is no one to keep alive the lore of the shrine of King Numa, and Rome will not be Rome anymore."

Demetria shook her head. "How strange to hear this from the murderer of Marcus!"

"He had a choice. His bravery was misplaced. It is..." Turanquil paused and seemed to swallow another word than the one that came out. "...regrettable."

"Regrettable, but necessary for you to have power over Rome. And then the lore! You want to destroy that, too."

"No," said Turanquil. "All this time we have merely been wishing to understand the lore. And to stop Lucius from destroying us. The Etruscans and the Romans must work hand in hand to make Rome great."

Demetria scoffed. "Hand in hand! You mean hand and

shackle! No *haruspica* I knew ever wanted Rome's good."

Turanquil blinked, and clenched her jaw. She was clearly trying to keep her patience. "It is well that you have spirit. But it has gotten you into trouble. You do not know how much."

"I have been in trouble before. Such as when you filled the *baculum* with gold. Is that a way to show that you mean well toward Rome?"

"Lucius is too young to use this thing. It is too powerful. He wishes to become king, and then, there is no end to what he might do with these grammarstones. Someone that young will make a terrible mistake."

Turanquil was speaking just reasonably enough to make Demetria think. She was right that he might be too young for the power of Numa if he continued to perfect grammars against those he loved! This thought made her hesitate, and she knew she was giving Turanquil an advantage. But it was difficult to know what to say.

Turanquil leaned forward in her chair. "Now," she said, not quite in a whisper, "you know that Lucius is in the Land of the Dead, seeking after the *baculum* that the goddess Vanth keeps in charge."

"He is allowed to seek after that which is Roman."

"But those who guard it will not allow him to take it."

Turanquil was right. Unless she wasn't. Was Lucius good enough? Without a *baculum* to throw the stones, could he defeat whatever was down in the depths?

The *haruspica* let Demetria stare at her for a moment before speaking again. "We will send you down. You will take this mirror." She brought the mirror out of her cloak again. As she had leaned forward, it was very close to Demetria. "This will allow us to see what you see, and it will give you power to defeat whatever is in your way. Simply hold the mirror up to your opponent, and it will destroy itself reflecting whatever attack it attempts."

Demetria's heart leapt. The mirror was a wondrous thing. The power of it was tempting. Her hand reached out for it, as if her hand had a mind of its own, but Turanquil drew it back.

"See," said Turanquil. She turned the mirror over to its non-reflective side. There was a scene of a beautiful goddess in flowing robes, attended by a host of winged graces, lithe goddesses who made women beautiful. To the side, a young man sat with his head down.

"Aphrodite!" Demetria said.

"Turan," Turanquil said. "And Atunis. See the young man who died." She took Demetria's hand, tapped the mirror with it where Atunis was.

Demetria pulled back her hand as if it had been stung, and rubbed it. Turanquil was talking about Adonis-- with whom Aphrodite fell in love, and who was gored by a wild boar while hunting. "Is that all you want, for me to persuade Lucius to come back?"

"Persuade him-- if he is not already dead," Turanquil said.

"And if I can't persuade him?"

"Then use the mirror. Trap him in the Mirror World. We can retrieve his spirit. It is a simple thing for a *haruspex* to do. He will be safe. You know he will."

"Just... make him look into it?"

"As you say."

"Not easy, I think," said Demetria.

"He trusts you. You will succeed. You know, as a

woman..." Turanquil smiled, as much as a *haruspica* could do. "It is something you can do when he is in your arms."

Demetria scowled. Did Turanquil know her so well? The mirror, with Turan and Atunis, the lovers. And what of the Shield? If she went after Lucius, the Shield would remain in the seers' hands, and they could do what they wanted with it. But without the summoning grammar, could she find it? Had Lucius been right after all?

But the mirror. The mirror changed everything.

With the mirror in her hands, regardless of who was carved on the back of it, she and he could defeat anything. It was stupid of Turanquil to trust her with it. As soon as she got it, she could trap Turanquil. She just needed to have the mirror in her hands.

Turanquil extended the bronze handle of the mirror to Demetria, but before Demetria could grasp it, she pulled it back. "You must vow, on the god you call Zeus, that you will never use it against me or any Etruscan. You will not destroy it, nor will you hide or lose it. And when your task is done, you will return it to me."

By Hercules! Demetria thought. Of course Turanquil would think of this. She must promise first.

"I do vow it," Demetria said quickly, and regretted it. She had not known of anyone who had been struck by lightning for breaking a vow made to Zeus, but she was not in the habit of breaking vows in any case. She had just made her job that much harder.

Turanquil gave her the mirror. "You will set out immediately, as soon as we can get you to the tomb chambers."

Demetria hefted the mirror in her hand. She was tempted

to look at her reflection, but knew that might end in disaster, with her in the Mirror World. "And the king knows nothing of this?"

"He does not know, and will not know. It is better to keep the things of *haruspices* and the things of rulership separate."

Demetria knew she had made a deal with the wrong person. There must be so many things Turanquil was not telling her. And Gnaeus! She could do nothing about him. But to have the mirror-- and to make sure Lucius did not die-- these were things she wanted. The shield, the grammar that homed the shield to the mage, both would have to wait.

::XVIII::

Demetria let her hand run along the hatched rim of the mirror as Turanquil spoke.

"If the king asks about you," she said, "We will use our mirrors to reflect back his words to him-- as if we are asking him. Thus he will be confused. We can do this for three days before he realizes the deception. You have that long to find Lucius and bring him back. If you do not, you must come yourself, or the king will know where you have gone.

"How will I know how many days I've been underground?" Demetria asked.

"We will give you enough food and water to be eaten in three days sparingly. When half the food and water is gone, turn back."

"Even if I have not found Lucius?"

"You will find him, or find evidence that he has lost his life."

Demetria shuddered.

They moved her out of her cell and took her to the main

corridor, where a slave met them with a bag of bread and a waterskin. With this over her shoulder and hanging next to the grammarstones, they took the staircase to the antechamber where Lucius had opened the three portals.

Turanquil went to the one with the *apanastar* priests and asked her to help. They pushed on the painted door, and the space began to move. The paint disguised that it was a real door, on hinges, made of wood, with a thin veneer of stone mortared over the wood.

"A beautiful trick!" Demetria declared, feeling the join between the stone and the wood.

Turanquil shushed her. "This is the place of the dead. Respect."

Demetria nodded, but continued to examine the secret door as they opened it wider. It revealed a passageway, tall enough to stand in, but not so tall that Turanquil could not touch the ceiling. The humid, faintly rotten smell of underground air filled Demetria's nostrils. The mirror began to glow in her hands, creating enough light to show a series of stairs, some carved, some natural rock.

"Take the stairs, and keep going," Turanquil said. "You will come to a river. Show the boatman your mirror, and he will let you pass. After that, beware, for there are many surprises we have no time to tell you about now. You will not find Lucius before you come to the river, because he took a different path, and may not have survived that one. In fact, it will have taken him much longer, so that you may catch up with him very soon. Not more than a day, I think."

Demetria extended the mirror so that the glow would illuminate more of the passage. Beyond the light, darkness. *I have gone below ground before*, she thought. *Nothing to be frightened of.*

"You are Greek," said Turanquil, as if she had heard her thoughts. "so you will think of many ways of surviving. We will be watching you. I would say good luck, as the Romans do, but for us *haruspices*, it is more a matter of reading the signs."

"And what do the signs say?"

"That you will die if you disobey my word," said Turanquil.

Demetria turned to go, but she felt Turanquil's hand on her shoulder. She turned back, and found herself staring into the woman's eyes.

"Use the mirror well, and it is yours," Turanquil assured her.

Demetria screwed up her mouth and gazed at the back side of the bronze disk, the slim, ghostly figures of Atunis and Turan.

"Yes," she said, and fled down the stairs without saying farewell.

For what seemed like a long time, Demetria descended in silence except for the scraping of her sandals. At first, the carved stairs made the going easy, and only in a few places did she have to jump a few feet from a natural outcropping to a landing, and then more stairs.

As she went, she wondered what she would say to Lucius when she met him, and that occupied her for some time. But then she stubbed her toe on an unseen rock, and the pain made her stop, and jarred her thoughts away from her friend. She sat down and rubbed her foot, wishing Turanquil had given her boots.

All at once she was impatient for the passageway to end, and the river to appear. How long? Not more than a day,

Turanquil had said. How long had she already gone?

Nothing to do but go down and find out.

The next stretch was more difficult. The stairs were not as well-carved, and the jumps from ledges longer. After a particularly tricky scramble down from a pile of rock almost as tall as she, and another stubbed toe, Demetria sat down to rest. Her feet were already smarting, and her knees and ankles starting to ache. She took out a piece of flatbread from the bag over her shoulder, to curtail her frustration more than her hunger.

The moist, yeasty smell of the bread-- it was still warm when the slave put it into the bag-- filled the chamber. Demetria tore a ribbon of it and ate, and the sound of her chewing seemed very loud in the near-dark. The sound filled her head, so that she seemed to hear nothing else except her sigh as the bread fed her spirit.

Until she heard something else.

She heard it while she was chewing her second bite. It almost sounded as if she was tapping her teeth. There was a skittering and a scraping, and she stopped chewing to listen. The skittering became something like a squeak, and the squeak something like a squawk. Then there was the sound of fluttering, as of wings.

Birds. Birds? Underground?

The sound grew rapidly louder, until, without warning, they were upon her. A flock of birds-- they looked like owls as they flew by-- that filled the lighted space above her, squawking and shrieking, their claws up, sharp beaks forward.

Demetria felt for a rock, grasped one, and flung it at one of the birds. It would've been a direct hit, but it passed directly through the bird, who continued to scream and show its claws.

Spirit birds! Demetria thought, and then realized, these are *striges*. Blood-sucking owls who came in the night, or so nurses would tell naughty children just before bed. "Be good, or the *striges* will get you," they would say. Lucius and his friends played *striges* many a day, a game of tag where one boy, playing the *strix*, would attempt to catch another, and if he did, that boy would become a *strix* as well, until all the boy *striges* were running after the lone survivor.

That's how Demetria felt now-- alone and chased. For some reason, the owls mostly kept their distance, but now and then one would swoop, peck, and attempt to claw. But when Demetria brought up the mirror to shield herself, she realized why the owls were being careful. Light flashed from the mirror. A *strix* disappeared.

"Beware the mirror, demons!" Demetria screamed in triumph, and the sound echoed through the passageway.

The *striges* continued to hover, but they did not attack, until they all did.

"By Hercules!" Demetria cried. It was as if she were in a swarm of bees. The owls made a cloud around her, and she waved the mirror here and there, but to no effect. She closed her eyes, and the glow of the mirror as she waved it made blue and purple ribbons on her mind's eye.

The *striges* began to peck and claw, but they did not wound like real bites and scrapes. Instead, she felt as if something cold and oozy was invading her inmost parts. She banged the mirror on the cave wall by accident, and the clanging sound made the birds retreat for a minute. Demetria examined the mirror for damage. A pit had been taken out of the reflective surface. She turned the mirror to the Turan side.

"Turan-- Aphrodite--" she prayed.

Then she remembered her grammarstones. She reached into the bag, and threw it as she spoke.

"*Striges-- non-- pugnans--*" She tried. *May the demon owls not be fighting.* Demetria realized as soon as she finished speaking that she had not made the grammar correctly. *Pugnans* should have been *pugnantes* to match with *striges*.

The owls did not stop fighting, though they avoided the stone as it flew, unlike the real stone. The grammarstone bounced off the wall, and impossibly, came flying back at Demetria. She only had time to pull up the mirror to try to block it.

The grammarstone hit the mirror with a clatter and almost knocked it out of Demetria's hands, wrenching her wrist. The mirror heated in an instant, and she had to drop it.

The mirror fell with the Turan side face up. And Demetria realized the stone had hit it on that side. The swan next to Turan was glowing bright-- almost white.

"*O anser pugnans striges!*" she cried. *I summon a swan fighting the demon owls.*

A white blur, a flurry of wings, and the deafening shrieks of the owls filled the passageway, along with a smell like hot metal. Demetria lay on the floor, put her arms over her head, and curled up her legs-- but parted two fingers on either side of an eye to let her see what was happening.

A hissing-- at first Demetria thought it came from the heated mirror-- came from the orange and black beak of the giant swan that had appeared, its long neck bobbing and striking at the spirit animals. Each time it struck, it hit one of the owls, and the owl disappeared with a squawk. In a few moments the *striges* were routed, flying down and away, back toward the Land of the Dead. Just as quickly, the swan disappeared as well, leaving faint light trails of its wings dancing on her eyes.

Demetria rose to a sitting position, tested the mirror with a finger. It was still hot. She would have to wait until it cooled. *Gladly will I wait!* she thought to herself. She was suddenly exhausted, hardly able to pick herself up from the gritty rock ledge. But tired as she was, she was happier still. She had used the mirror, and perfected a grammar, and there was nothing better than that.

A mouthful of water and the rest of the bread helped her regain her strength. The mirror cooled. She turned it over and over to examine it. There was still the pit in the reflecting side, which she hoped would not affect its power, and on the picture side, the swan was now only a warm, uncarved mass, like wax.

"Can I never summon my swan again?" she thought with regret. She waited, feeling the mirror now and then as it cooled, and when it was, replaced it in the fold of her cloak and resumed her descent.

::XIX::

The staircase went up for such a long time that Lucius finally had to stop to catch his breath, and he realized that he was tired, hungry, and thirsty. Could he steal a few moments of sleep in this place? He knew he could summon food and drink with a grammarstone-- he had done it before, when in caverns of the prodigies-- but he only knew one way to rest.

He sat down with his back against the wall, and thought he would stay there for only a few moments. But his first mistake was to sit down at all.

He woke to complete darkness, first thinking that he must be home in his bed. But swiftly he realized the truth when he tried to move, and his limbs stiffened from long sleep on rocks.

"I was so tired I needed neither pillow nor mattress!" Lucius thought. He quickly made grammar light, and the passageway lit up, much the same as it had been before.

He had no idea how long he'd slept, but it might have been hours, because he was refreshed. He had not dreamed that he remembered, and the memory of the larva was not as strong or as terrifying.

"*O panis et aqua magistro mago*," he said, naming bread and water so that he could restore himself. It appeared in his hands, and a grammarstone disappeared in return. He never could keep a grammarstone that he had used to summon things.

Having eaten and drunk, he moved on, up the stairs, and within an hour he was limber again, and going at a good pace. Soon, as if the gods were rewarding him, the passageway opened, and he came into a series of caverns with openings between.

Now the going was slower, as he had to find the doors between the caverns, some of them small and nearly hidden, but this kind of work kept Lucius' spirits up, for he felt he must be getting closer to his goal. After hours of this, he again sat down, made bread and water, and then went on again, never meeting anyone, whether spirit or human.

Not long after his rest and food, he finally came to a great cavern with an underground river flowing by.

The cavern walls rose higher than the light, which meant he might fly over the river using a grammar. He could also summon a boat, or stepping-stones if the water was shallow.

Or he could use the boat that was already there.

Lucius had put his grammar light a few arms' lengths in front of him, and it moved to the left or right as he turned his head. Once on the shore of the river, which was much smaller than the Tiber, and silent, though it did flow, Lucius looked downriver to see a boat, shallow bottomed and turned up like a fallen leaf, moored to an outcropping of rock on the other bank.

No one was with the boat, but no doubt it was used to ferry passengers across the river. Lucius thought of the stories of the Greek underworld he had heard from Demetria-- of the boatman, Charon, who ferried souls across the River Styx if they had been buried with a coin closing their eyes, and could pay the toll.

Charon. But that was a Greek story. This was the Etruscan Land of the Dead.

If Lucius could get across the river without using a grammar, he would have more stones to use later. He picked up a largish rock to test the depth of the water. Plunk! There was a splash, and then nothing. It could be very deep.

The cavern wall came down directly to the riverbank both up and downriver. Lucius would not be able to walk along the bank to find a narrower place.

Across, then. But how?

In the end, he decided to hold a grammarstone in his hand and fly over the river. He would not lose a stone that way, and he would not disturb the boat or its owner, whoever that was.

"*Magus magister vento altera ripa fluminis,*" he said. *May the master mage be on the other side of the river, by the wind.*

A gust came up and rippled the surface of the water, and then Lucius was borne off his feet.

Just as quickly, however, another gust of wind came up, and pushed against the wind that was carrying Lucius across. For a moment he was suspended over the middle of the river, with the competing winds making a deafening roar in his ear, and buffeting against him and making his cloak whip, and then the contrary wind won, and Lucius was pushed back to the riverbank again.

Lucius opened his palm. The grammarstone he had used was gone.

At the same time, across the river, the rope mooring the boat to the boulder slipped off and dropped into the water with a quiet splash. Then, like a water snake, it rose again by itself and pulled its length into the boat. Now free, the boat began moving across the river, against the current.

Lucius took out his sling, deposited a grammarstone in it, and said, "*Spiritus scaphae visus*," *may the spirit in the boat be visible.*

A shape began to form in the boat, of a truly horrible creature. It was larger than a man, broad-shouldered, with huge wings, a face like the cross between a wild boar and a wild man. Tusks came from his gaping mouth; his nose was a snout, and his eyes shining and angry. His hair was mixed gray and black, down to its shoulders, with things like beetles crawling in it. He was armored with a helmet and breastplate, but the bronze and leather were spoiled, rusting. His skin was blue and in places eaten away by worms.

The monster stood in the back of the boat, using an enormous hammer as a paddle, dipping it first on one side, then the other of the flat-bottomed boat.

For a time, it kept itself busy with paddling, but as soon as it looked up, and saw the Lucius could see it, it roared with anger, and its wings spread out behind it and flapped.

Lucius was chilled. He grabbed a grammarstone and pulled his sling from his cloak. Something-- a spear, fire, he didn't know what-- was going to come from that stone. But he wasn't going to let the monster swing that hammer against him.

As the monster came closer, Lucius realized he was muttering something, and it was in Etruscan. Lucius understood perfectly because his mother had spoken Etruscan to him as a child, and often still did.

"Pay the toll, pay the toll," it was saying.

Then he knew the monster was Charon, but an Etruscan kind, and that Lucius had no coin with him and wasn't a spirit in any case. What would the monster do? Take a toll of Lucius' life first?

Lucius knew this type of thing-- for it was an Etruscan god-- would not be affected by physical fire or spears, for it was a spirit, though it appeared the hammer was real enough. Instead, Lucius thought, perhaps something else would work.

"*Sonus defunctorum ripa fluminis*," he said, and slung a grammarstone upriver. *The sounds of the dead on the bank of the river.* If indeed this Charon was a carrier of dead souls across this river, he would be interested in those distant sounds.

Across the face of the river came a murmuring-- a murmuring in Etruscan. "*We must pass the river, we must pass the river*," it said.

Charon's wings spread again, and his pointed ears flexed. He looked up toward the sound.

"They are waiting," whispered Lucius in Etruscan.

Charon eye's bored into Lucius' for a moment, but then he was in the air, his great wings flapping, the hammer clutched in both hairy hands. The boat lingered in the slow current, then began to drift downstream. Charon flew away, and in a moment was gone.

Magus magister vento scaphae: May the master mage be in the boat on the wind.

The gust of wind came again and swept him up, lightly depositing him in the center of the boat just vacated by

Charon. The boat sagged, and water trickled in over the gunwales, pooling in the bottom, but it did not sink. Lucius steadied himself, then knelt on the center bench, and held the gunwales on each side. There was no way to guide the boat without a paddle, but Lucius leaned over and pushed the water with his hand to nose the boat toward the other bank. It was not far. He could get there just by drifting, Lucius thought.

But then, almost as soon as he took his hand out of the water, the current began to speed up.

Lucius had never been on a boat in a rushing river, though he had seen the Tiber running fast over rocks when the water was low. This was new. He sat down on the bench and held it with both hands. The river was not descending quicker, nor was it going over rocks. It seemed as if the water itself had sped up of its own accord.

The boat lurched forward and spun. The water lapped up against the cave walls on the right, and on the rocky ground of the cavern on the left. Before long the river curved to the left, and the boat strayed close to the right bank, but before Lucius could grasp the wall, the wash of water against it pushed the boat back into the center. Lucius held on, unable to think of a grammar that might stop the ride, and hoping that it might end by bringing him closer to his destination, though he hardly knew where that was.

In the next quarter hour, the river jogged two or three times in the same way that it had, and Lucius understood that it was curving as if running in a circle. Once he saw an opening in the cavern wall on the right, similar to the one he had taken to get there. He began to understand: the river must run completely around the Land of the Dead, and the boatman must travel along the river picking up souls. No one could get into the Land of the Dead without crossing the river.

If Lucius was going in a circle, then that meant he would eventually come back to where he had been-- and Charon would meet him as well.

If not-- well, he would find out.

In less time than it had taken than before, the current began to run even faster. What was ahead? Was it simply that somehow the river running in a circle could speed up or slow down as it wished, or as Charon bid it?

The grammar light told him the answer-- too late. The river widened out into a pool-- but not just a pool. The water was swirling in a circle, an ever-tightening circle that was dropping into a hole in the center of the pool.

In a few circles, Lucius and the boat would disappear down that vortex.

Lucius grabbed a grammarstone and threw it toward the center of the pool. "*Flumen immotus.*" *May the river be still.*

Nothing. The river continued to swirl. Lucius had no time to think, just threw another stone and yelled, "*O saxum caviti flumen-- maximum.*" *I summon a rock in the hole of the river-- a huge one.*

It was a desperate grammar, and Lucius knew it. When a rumbling sounded from above, and an enormous cone of rock fell from the ceiling, Lucius could only shield his eyes. The rock fell directly into the middle of the whirlpool and hit bottom with a terrible, bone-wrenching shudder.

The boat continued to rotate for a brief time, but then, as water filled the vortex, it calmed, and Lucius peeked over the side. The waves met in the center, slapped and pushed away from each other. The boat crept closer to the Land of the Dead side.

Then, before Lucius could even begin to think about jumping to shore, there came an even bigger shudder, followed by a crack. Water boiled to the surface and sprayed out from the center. Lucius was borne up on a wave and hurtled out of the boat and into the dark. There was no way he could grasp a grammarstone, no time to think. He was spun end over end, and in that instant of time he was airborne, he was able to say one prayer:

May Demetria be able to do for Rome all that I couldn't.

He didn't address any particular god. He hadn't time to think about which one might be listening. But just after he finished, he felt a terrible snag in his cloak and a wrenching of his body. He stopped flipping; he seemed to float for a moment. The dark was total, and then it wasn't. In the near distance he made out what looked like a glowing disk with a handle, like a frying pan. The light was orange, and gave off a glow that illuminated a small bubble of space below him.

Wings beat above him. He looked up. In the dimmest glow of the faintest orange light, he made out a boar snout and tusks below the wings.

Charon.

::XX::

Walking helped Demetria regain strength in her legs after the *striges*. The mirror stayed warm and gave its orangish light, and she felt along the pit in the surface of the mirror. When she put her finger directly into the indentation, her whole arm buzzed, and her bicep went gooseflesh.

"I will have someone repair this when I return," she thought. "I will keep it-- Turanquil will let me."

Thinking about how she might keep and use the mirror once she got back aboveground occupied her thoughts for a time, but soon she had to concentrate on the way ahead: the stairs ended, and now there were only rock ledges of increasing size. On the wall above one of the ledges, Etruscan script was carved.

"Looks like Greek," said Demetria, who had seen her father's account scrolls. "But gods help me if I had to tell what it says."

Then she thought of something. She stood on tiptoe and extended the mirror to the script, so that they faced each other.

In Demetria's head she could hear, "This is the Place of Vanth. Welcome to the spirits who enter, but to the living, turn back or die."

"I don't know if I wanted to know this!" she thought, but nevertheless marveled at what the mirror could do.

She scrambled down a couple more ledges, scraping her bare knees and elbows, before coming to a cavern with something like a floor. It looked as if it had been carved out more carefully than the preceding passageway, and there were paintings on all sides.

In front of her, above the threshold to the stairs, two leopards were painted, so lifelike they seemed to be jumping out of the wall at her.

And then they were.

They leapt so fast that Demetria only heard a snarl before one of them bowled her over. The mirror flew out of her hands as she tried to break her fall. Hot fangs bite into her neck.

She screamed in pain, rolling on her back. The leopard dugs its claws in and bit again. She rolled over the mirror, scooped it up, and brought it down hard on what she thought was the leopard's head.

There was a shrieking caterwaul, and the weight of the leopard disappeared. In fact, the leopard itself disappeared.

Demetria had time to touch her neck and feel the wetness and punctures before the second leopard leapt. This time she ducked, held onto the mirror, and the leopard flashed by.

The cat crouched as if to leap again, but Demetria squared herself in front of it, bent her knees, and held the reflecting face of the mirror out toward it.

"For Rome and Greece!" she cried, and rushed toward the leopard, mirror cocked and ready to strike.

The cat was much faster. It backed away, snarled, and met the mirror with a thrust of its paw. The force of the blow spun Demetria around. Dizzy, she saw nothing for a moment, and then teetered, fell, and rolled.

"Hold on to the mirror!" she whispered hotly to herself.

The leopard half-snarled and half-howled as it leapt. Demetria turned over just in time to see yellow eyes, whiskers, and fangs fill her vision.

Then she saw the bronze face of Turan, the mirror shuddered, and flew out of Demetria's hand. It clattered away and went end over end down several of the steps beyond the threshold.

Beyond?

Demetria sat up. There were no more leopards. No one to stop her-- or the mirror-- from going down the stairs.

She dusted off her knees and looked up to the space above the threshold. No leopards.

But when she picked up the mirror and checked its condition, she noticed, in the glow of it, that the head of a cat had been added in the background of the Turan scene.

"Farewell, Master Leopard," she said, and wiped her brow. "I hope you find the spirit world to your liking."

The bites of the first leopard stung, but fortunately were not deep punctures. She took a few minutes to catch her breath and gather her spirit before going on. When she did, her legs still felt as soft as rotten cucumbers, and she stopped and rested several times, trying to clear the vision of the yellow eyes and fangs from her mind.

Perhaps a half hour more of hard descent finally brought her to a place that Lucius would've well recognized if they had been together-- the river of Charon.

There was no boat here, and Demetria had no idea of how to get across, but soon Charon appeared, responding to Lucius' grammar of souls wishing passage across the river.

Demetria would have run at the sight of the boatman, but her legs were nearly useless, and before she even had the chance to bring up her mirror in defense, Charon floated down to her, furled his wings, and bowed on one knee.

"LADY," he croaked in Etruscan, pointing to the mirror.

Another victory for the mirror! Demetria thought.

"I seek a boy," said Demetria, speaking Etruscan also, for like all merchant's children, she knew the languages of the people who were her father's customers. "I wish him safe. Can you help me?"

"ROMAN," Charon said, and the rumble in his voice said that he didn't much like the idea of saving a Roman boy.

"Bring me to him, if you know where he is."

Charon nodded, and pointed with his hammer to his shoulders. He brought the hammer forward, and she understood she could use it as a stepstool. When she reached out for his wing, her hand went straight through him. But in the same moment, she felt herself borne up.

Charon beat his wings, and Demetria was sitting on his shoulders. She felt nothing-- and yet felt as secure as if she were mounted a strong, tall, horse.

"By all the gods," she whispered, "and the God of Everything!"

They rose. The wind from the wings slapped against

Demetria's face. She clutched the mirror, and the cavern walls lit up like fire.

Demetria could not see below her-- the light didn't extend that far-- but was glad they were flying, because as they went, they passed through clouds of foul smoke that smelled like rotten eggs, and the sound of boiling and quaking.

Worse, columns of heat rose that made sweat bead on her temples.

Before she could fully imagine how difficult it would have been to walk from the river and their destination, a sound came to her ears of some kind of water flowing, as quiet at first as if someone was saying "hush" over and over.

The sound grew as they came near it, until it filled her ears with its roaring. Charon lit on a flat rock next to the river, which was now hastening down a hole in a tremendous whirlpool.

"Where is the boy?" Demetria asked after she had scrambled down from Charon's shoulders-- it was like dismounting a cloud.

In almost the same moment, a light appeared upriver, much brighter than the mirror light, and whiter. In it, Demetria caught sight of Lucius, crouched in a small boat and holding on to the gunwales with both hands.

Demetria was about to cry out, but Lucius threw a grammarstone at the whirlpool. Shortly after that, there was a groan, a crack, and a cone-shaped boulder fell from the roof into the center of the hole.

"Lucius!" Demetria screamed. "You did it!"

At first the water slowed, and Lucius went about the pool in a circle once. He seemed to have no idea that Demetria or

Charon were there, and he certainly did not when the stone at the bottom of the water cracked in two and the water threw Lucius into the air.

"Get him!"

But Charon had taken flight even before she spoke, and caught Lucius by the ends of his cloak. His sandal dangled from his toe, one of the straps broken.

Lucius' cloak tore. Demetria screamed.

::XXI::

"Lucius!"

"Demetria?"

"You're safe!"

Lucius Junius Brutus leaned against a boulder to steady himself. He examined in turn the long tear in his cloak, then Charon, who stood near, and finally, Demetria, who was holding a glowing Etruscan mirror that limned her dirty, beautiful face from below.

For the tiniest space of time, he hesitated, and so did she. But in the end, he let go of the boulder, took a step toward her, and she made up the difference.

They held on for a long time, and Lucius felt strength and hope and confidence welling up in him, as if his genius was blessing him. But when he finally let her go, and she him, Demetria's face reminded him of the sea on a gray, windy day.

"I'm sorry," he said, looking into her eyes. "I shouldn't have."

She shook her head. "I understand. Marcus was...

everything to you. But--"

A scraping sound came from beside them. They both swiveled their necks. It was Charon, dragging his hammer on the stone like an "ahem." It was clear he was a spirit, but able to hold things-- including a master mage flying through the air, and to set him down safely at the order of the "Etruscan" mistress with the mirror.

Demetria held up the mirror, asked Charon to wait, and finished her sentence. "Never do it again."

"Never," Lucius said.

And the trouble on Demetria's face melted.

Lucius turned to Charon and said, in Etruscan, "Thank you."

Charon nodded toward Demetria. "MIRROR," he rumbled. "LADY."

Demetria held the mirror up triumphantly. "This saved you! Charon respects it mightily. He thinks I am a *haruspica*."

"But how--"

"They sent me. Turanquil. She gave-- leant-- me the mirror, to get you to come back without the *baculum*."

Lucius eyed her. It was a lot to take in after flying through the air and being saved by an Etruscan underworld demon.

"Even now they see us. The mirror allows this." She ran her hand along the reflective side of the mirror. "But I would have died without it."

"Why..." Lucius' hand went to his forehead. "Whyever would you take that? The blood on it. My brother's."

"She didn't use *this* mirror. It was a dagger that..."

"No," Lucius burst out.

"Don't, Lucius," Demetria said. "Not again."

A tear of frustration ran down Lucius' cheek. This was too much. Too much to take, too much to do. *You are a master mage!* he heard Logo say in his heart. *A master mage who perfects grammar against those he loves!* Another voice said.

Too much! Lucius fell onto one knee, squeezing his eyelids tight. In the darkness of his mind's eye, the world seemed to reel.

Then it was so quiet the only sound was the swish of the river and a low grumbling from Charon, who finally said, "LADY."

"A moment more!" Demetria cried. She knelt next to Lucius. "It's all right, you know. We can go back up to the light. I know the way."

A faint whisper. "Is that what they want?"

"Yes. Lucius, they sent me to take you back, but I went because I was afraid for your life. And the mirror-- well, if I hadn't come, and Charon hadn't been there..."

"I would have died."

Demetria set the mirror down and put an arm over Lucius' shoulder. "You are safe. Isn't that enough?"

Lucius opened his eyes. The first thing he saw was the mirror on the ground, the sculpted mounds of metal glinting dully.

"You are done with this thing," he said. "Cast it away."

"I promised I wouldn't. And we need it. To get back."

"My grammarstones are not enough?"

"In the Etruscan Land of the Dead, the mirror is powerful."

Lucius considered. Demetria's arm over his shoulder soothed his spirit, yet a stubbornness remained. "We need to get the *baculum*," he said.

"We need to find the Shield, too."

"First, the *baculum*. We are here now." Lucius stood up, motioned around him.

Charon rumbled again.

"But the Shield is important. They have it. Who knows what they will do with it?"

"But I-- you-- we have come so far. Do you want to turn back?" But Lucius knew the answer. She'd come to fetch him, not to help him get the *baculum*. Could it be that the Shield was more important? Something-- a spirit, perhaps his genius speaking to him?-- nagged.

"Lucius."

Charon said, "LADY."

"You see? He wants us to go back. We're alive, after all, not spirits. We shouldn't be down here."

Now Charon spoke even louder. "LADY!"

Demetria looked up, and Lucius turned to see what had caught her attention. There, in the radiance of the mirror, was a thing even taller than Charon. It had two arms and two legs, but its face was horrible. It had donkey's ears, the beak of a vulture, and a mane that circled its face, made completely of serpents, some of which coiled round its muscular arms.

Lucius fell, his knees giving way. He scrambled back to where Demetria had crouched, and he felt in his bag for grammarstones, though his stomach had gone into knots and he didn't know whether he could speak a word, much less think of a grammar.

Demetria picked up the mirror again, and said in Etruscan, "We wish to go back. Charon will take us."

Lucius thought she had done well even to say as much as she did, but the thing shook its head, and put its huge arms over its chest. The snakes hissed and one of them uncoiled toward the two youths.

"By Hercules!" Lucius gasped. "I know this creature. From the tomb of my great aunt. It is Tuchulcha, Vanth's servant. We are close, very close to her." Realizing what the creature was had given him a strange courage, and a renewed desire to seek the *baculum*-- if this thing would let them, or could be defeated.

Demetria held out the mirror. "Withdraw the snake, or it will be destroyed," she said. Her voice shook and so did her hand, but the mirror seemed to glow brighter as the snake advanced.

"I warn you," Demetria said, knees bent and holding the reflecting side of the mirror away from her.

The mirror flashed. The snake hissed, but withdrew.

"Well done, Demetria!" Lucius cried. Now Lucius had his hand on a grammarstone, and was thinking hard what could defeat this monster in one sentence. But his mind was working quickly, and he discarded the first idea for a second one: "We seek Vanth," he said.

"What?" Demetria blurted.

Tuchulcha looked down at Lucius and seemed to study him for a moment. The snakes also seemed to bend towards him. The demon then caught Charon's eye, and extended an arm, pointing back with a claw the way he and Demetria had come.

Charon nodded, unfurled his wings, lifted off the ground, and was gone.

"Lucius, what are you doing? Charon-- he was our friend,

he could have helped!"

"We're so close, Demetria. Tuchulcha can lead us to her."

Tuchulcha now pointed in the opposite direction, beckoning the two youths to follow him.

"Will we see Vanth?" Lucius asked.

The snakes hissed as one, and Tuchulcha waved his arm, calling to them.

"This one speaks even less than Charon," Demetria said. "What if he is leading us to our deaths?"

"Let's go," Lucius said. "He could have already killed us. Or he is afraid of your mirror! Hold it out to him, and I will have a grammarstone ready."

Demetria gave Lucius a hard stare. "Lucius Junius, you truly are Brutus."

He didn't answer, but took her hand, and they followed Tuchulcha into the depths of the Land of the Dead.

::XXII::

Lucius had to do more shuffling than walking because of the broken strap on his sandal, but he and Demetria kept pace with Tuchulcha as he half-walked, half-floated in front of them. His feet fell noiselessly on the stone, in contrast to the slap of the youth's sandals on the cavern floor.

"Turanquil is not going to be pleased," said Demetria. "If you had come with me, we could have made it seem I was obeying her, and we could have found the Shield."

Lucius said nothing, but squeezed her hand and hoped his decision had been a good one. He was grateful that she did not try to let go.

Soon, they came to the foot of a stony slope. Stairs had been cut into it. The stairs went straight up. They were tightly cut, inlaid with jewels and lapis lazuli on the edge of the risers. They shone and sparkled in the mirror light.

Tuchulcha pointed upwards.

At the top of the stairs, up so far that they almost couldn't see, there was some kind of threshold. Demetria passed the mirror over her head, and the light bounced off of a glittering bronze, highly polished door.

"Vanth is there?" Lucius asked.

Tuchulcha gave the slightest of nods, and turned away from the stairs toward two rocks close to one another, with flat tops, in front of a wall that was spattered dark brown.

"Is it blood?" Lucius wondered. Demetria's silence told him she didn't want to guess.

Tuchulcha motioned to one of the rocks.

Lucius came forward and sat.

Tuchulcha then traced a claw along the blots of brown on the wall. He made a cup of his other hand, and pretended to drink.

"Wine?" Lucius said. "Do you mean wine?"

Tuchulcha sat down next to him, and it was all Lucius could do to remain sitting, with the snakes coiling about the huge monster's arms. Tuchulcha made a motion as if he was throwing something against the wall.

"By all the gods! I know what he means," Demetria said. "It's that game. My father plays it at drinking parties and boasts at dinner about his prowess in it."

"*Kottabus*," said Lucius. "That's the name of the game. I tried as well with my friends-- with water. But why...?" He couldn't imagine what a monster would want to do with such a game.

Tuchulcha nodded at the word *kottabus* and extended his hand to Lucius' grammarstone bag.

Lucius clutched the bag. Tuchulcha made a sign of drinking again.

"There is no wine in this bag, Tuchulcha," Lucius said.

"But there is!" Demetria said. "He must know you can summon it."

Tuchulcha made a crow's croak and nodded.

"I still don't--" Lucius said, but he reached into his bag, took out a stone, and said, "*O vinum poculo.*" *I summon wine in a cup.*

It was in his hand, a bronze-stemmed, brimming goblet.

The smell of the wine quickly filled the space: a rich, living smell that reminded Lucius of late summer and fall, when the harvest came in, and the grapes were crushed, and all of Rome smelled like a berry. The memory calmed him, and though the snakes hissed and Tuchulcha's beak clacked, Lucius felt stronger than he had since entering the Land of the Dead.

Tuchulcha nodded at the wall, and a lampstand appeared, almost as tall as Lucius standing. A figurine-- maybe half a foot in height-- was balanced on the lampstand, clearly a man.

"What is that?" Demetria asked. She went forward, picked it up. Tuchulcha made no movement.

"It is Nauarchus," she said. "A more beautiful likeness than ever I've seen. It is wondrous!" She replaced the figurine on the stand

Tuchulcha waved her away, and again made the throwing motion.

"He wants us to play," Lucius said. "To knock down the figurine. But what are the stakes?"

Tuchulcha pointed to the statue of Nauarchus, then to the both of them, and motioned up the stairs.

"He must be saying if you can knock Nauarchus off the stand, you can go in to Vanth's chamber," Demetria said.

"But if I do, what happens then?" Lucius turned to

Tuchulcha. "What do you win?"

Tuchulcha pointed at the statue, then used the same claw to draw a line across his own neck. His snakes hissed as one.

"Nauarchus?" Demetria cried, letting the mirror fall to her side. "You can take his soul?"

Tuchulcha nodded.

"No," said Lucius, and Demetria said "Never" almost at the same time.

Tuchulcha croaked and extended his hand toward the grammarstone bag.

Lucius stood up. "You can't take them," he said. "Try, and be punished."

Tuchulcha croaked again. Quick as thought, a snake struck. But not Lucius.

Demetria, while her guard was down.

"Ah!" she cried, as the snake sunk its fangs into her arms, cutting through her cloak. She fell, and the mirror fell with her. The light went crazily about the cavern as it rolled on its side and then hit the handle and lay flat.

Tuchulcha now made the throwing motion again, and the snakes hissed, bobbing up and down as they did.

Lucius shook his head. Was Demetria dead? She seemed not to be breathing-- or only very slowly. "You. You have to revive her," he said through clenched teeth. He was hot and cold at the same time, his flesh chilled but his heart pounding crazily. "If I win, you have to bring her back."

Tuchulcha swiveled toward the wall, and the snakes quieted.

Lucius sat down again. Tuchulcha hadn't nodded. But those must be the stakes. Shaken, he steadied his gaze on the statue of Nauarchus. Everything had gone wrong! There was nothing left to do but play. But what would be the outcome-- Nauarchus' death? But Demetria! He stared at her, then at Tuchulcha, and took the wine cup, waiting until his hand was steady enough to hold it.

"For Demetria," he whispered, his heart still aflame.

Tuchulcha tensed. It was clear he truly wanted to see the game played. The stains on the wall showed he had played it before.

The cup of wine was too full for a good throw, so Lucius poured out a little. Tuchulcha grunted, and a snake descended to the ground where the wine had spilled. Licking it at with its forked tongue, Tuchulcha cocked his head and said something that sounded like *mmmmm*.

Lucius threw. The wine flew in a jet toward the Nauarchus figurine, hitting it, making it move, but not making it fall down. Some of the wine spattered on the wall.

Now, perhaps a third of the liquid remained in the cup, not enough for a good throw, so he summoned more. The smell of the wine came again, filling his head, steadying his spirit.

"You shall not take Demetria," he told Tuchulcha. How strange a game this was-- he would have laughed to see the fearsome monster waiting patiently for the next throw, if that throw were not about to determine life or death.

Lucius threw again. This time he missed cleanly and painted a long, clean vertical line of wine on the rock behind the lamp stand. He gasped for air-- he had been holding his breath-- and the picture of Nauarchus' face came to him. *Surely he cannot!* he thought, and then *What am I doing?*

Tuchulcha made a deep croaking rumble in his throat, and

held up two claws.

"Two," said Lucius. "Two throws, is that what you mean? And I get one more? Or do you mean two deaths, perhaps? Demetria and me if I miss, and Nauarchus lives? But if I knock him down, he perishes! So whatever happens, you have at least one soul."

Tuchulcha nodded very slowly, turning his claws over to motion to the figurine.

For the first time, Lucius thought of the idea that if Nauarchus died, then Demetria would not have to marry him. If he knocked over the figurine, Demetria would be restored to him, and Nauarchus--

"No!" he said aloud, and Tuchulcha grunted. Snakes raised their heads.

Lucius threw-- but not wine.

"*Statua Graeci statua monstri facta!*" he called out as he threw. *May the statue of the Greek be made a statue of the monster.* The grammarstone he'd reached for and let go hit the statue square, and made a spark. Then Lucius let the wine go, almost in the same motion as he had the stone. The wine doused the spark, and the figurine tottered and fell to the ground.

The room was filled with a smell like burnt honey, like a cake that had been in a brick oven too long.

Tuchulcha rose, and seemed to give a kind of monstrous chuckle deep in his throat, a rumble of satisfaction. His snakes hissed one by one in succession, making a kind of ha-ha-ha-ha-ha.

Demetria stirred. "Nauarchus," she moaned.

But Lucius ran to the figurine and picked it up. "Wait! See." He held out the figurine to Tuchulcha. "This is not Nauarchus

I knocked down."

Tuchulcha opened his beak and let out a deep croak, like a crow that has to move away from the carcass it has been scavenging.

"Look! It is Tuchulcha."

It was indeed Tuchulcha, a perfect likeness in bronze.

Tuchulcha roared in anger, and Lucius took a step back, but kept his gaze fixed on the monster. His grammar had worked, thanks be to Egeria!

Demetria raised her head, but seemed to see nothing.

"I won," said Lucius. "It is you who must yield to me."

"Phane?" Demetria said dreamily. "Phane? Where are you? I feel ill. Phane?"

Tuchulcha straightened up. A wind stirred, taking with it the smell of the burnt wine. It strengthened, enough to bend Lucius over and hold on to his stone seat, and it seemed to take Tuchulcha with it. He began to fade-- like a true spirit that can be seen through.

The monster waved farewell, and disappeared.

::XXIII::

Demetria was having a dream that she was home. But it was a strange dream, because instead of Phane bending over her to wake her up, it was Lucius. Could they be married?

"By the God of Everything!" Demetria cried, sitting up straight. The thought had not only woken her up, it had filled her with a fear that was almost a wish.

"*Arana Melana!*" Lucius cried. *Hello, Friend.*

No, they weren't married. They were still in the Etruscan Land of the Dead.

"Oh, thank the gods!" Demetria found herself saying, and wrapped herself around Lucius' neck. It was the only time she'd ever felt relieved to be in a cavern instead of her own bed.

When she let go, Lucius asked if she was hurt. She showed him the twin punctures of the snake's bite.

"Does it hurt?"

Demetria flexed her arm. "Not as much as it should! This is the third time I've been bitten today! First *striges*, then leopards, now a snake. And I am still alive!"

"What a tale that will make!" Lucius said. "But let's not hope for a fourth bite."

"No fear of that!" Demetria said with a laugh. "But what happened?"

Lucius told her, and she said, "Well done! If only I had been awake. I was dreaming that I was home. But you were there, and that didn't make sense!"

Lucius smiled. "We will have our own house someday," he said.

Demetria found she liked that, but Lucius was bound to say anything after the fright they'd had.

He motioned up to the stairs before them. "Are you ready?" He squeezed Demetria's hand again.

"We've come this far."

Demetria tried to stand, found she could, but before they started, they both had a drink from Demetria's water skin. She also poured a little over her face.

"I feel almost alive," she said, and sighed.

"Remember, we are not souls to be escorted to our ancestors! Don't let Vanth give you that thought."

It was almost as if they were playing next to the Tiber rather than about to meet the Etruscan goddess of death.

It took some effort to get to the top. The stairs were steep, and Demetria got out of breath a couple of times. But they found their way to the bronze double doors. Lucius checked them, found they were barred, held a grammarstone to the door and perfected a grammar to slide the bar to the side. There was a groaning of metal on metal as the bar slid. The doors parted, and Demetria pushed one side and Lucius the other.

"A wonder," Demetria whispered. The room was another cavern, but lit with torches, and noticeably warm. Torches were fixed into almost every crevice of the stone walls. The light was dazzling at first, and the smell of burning pitch, that covered the torches, immediately filled her nostrils.

No ceiling bounced the light back at them. The cavern seemed to rise forever.

In front of them, there was a raised platform, made of chiseled marble, and inlaid with gold. On the top of it, a chest, shining black, perhaps made of wood, or stone, or something else. The chest was not long, a bit more than half the height of a tall man, and only a foot or so tall and wide.

"Just big enough for a *baculum*," Lucius said.

Opposite them, on the far wall, a door with the *dokana* posts, the same kind that led from the mirror world to the real one in their previous adventure. The outlines of twin warriors, incisions filled with gold, guarded each side of a bronze door.

"There's no one here," Demetria said. The empty room gave her a strange feeling. It wasn't as if something was going to leap out at them. It was as if this was a sacred place where no one came, perhaps even a forgotten place.

Lucius must not have been thinking the same. "Beware everything here. It's likely to come to life at any moment." And he motioned at the twins.

Demetria nodded, and thought of the leopards. "Perhaps, and perhaps not. It is odd, but I feel as if we must have come through all the defenses-- that now we are 'inside' rather than trying to find a way in."

"May you speak truly, by all the gods!" Lucius said, and his words echoed through the cavern, flying about like the spirits of the dead. He turned to the platform again. "Logo said the chest holding the *baculum* had no lid nor lock, and that I would have to find a grammar to open it."

"Maybe an axe would be a better tool."

"With a goddess, maybe we should ask first."

Demetria ventured a stroll around the chamber, eyes moving from the torches to the chest and back again. "She might be out collecting souls. We might take the chest and leave before she comes back. Ouch!"

The mirror had heated in her hand, and Demetria dropped it. It fell on the Turan side, and a spot of orange glowed much brighter than the rest of the mirror. Out of that bright spot the metal boiled and hissed, and from it, so fast they couldn't see how, a dove flew up, beating its wings to perch on the chest.

It was a turtledove, grayish-brown, with eyes like the blackest, shiniest pebbles Demetria had ever seen. Its trunk was fat and round, its feathers soft and perfectly in place.

"Beautiful," was all Demetria could say.

"My mother had a pet bird like that," Lucius said. "Many Etruscans do."

"You want to take it in your hand and stroke its neck," said Demetria.

"It came from the mirror," Lucius said.

Demetria tested the mirror with a finger, found it wasn't hot anymore, and picked it up. "The place where-- see--" she showed it to Lucius "--there used to be a winged grace."

She was right. Just as with the swan next to Turan, one of the winged goddesses was now gone, and in its place a smudge of melted metal.

"That one cannot be Vanth," said Lucius. "In Etruria the grace is called Lasa."

"Goddesses come in many guises," Demetria said. "Maybe she will help."

But then, again seemingly out of nowhere, there came the sound of paws on stone-- the clicking of claws-- and Kaneesh appeared.

"Kaneesh! Stranger and stranger!" Lucius said. "Where did you come from?"

Demetria looked up into the darkness. "There must be a way out of here that we do not know-- maybe one that goes from here to the shrine."

The dove cooed. Previously it had been silent, but now it made the *prrr prrrr* sound characteristic of doves. Kaneesh sat down next to Lucius and panted, and as Lucius passed his hand over her head and ears in greeting, she gave a little bark.

The dove ruffled its feathers, and stood up on its feet, but continued to coo, and then began walking over the surface of the chest.

Kaneesh barked again, and the dove flew up, startled, but then lit on the chest again. Kaneesh stood up, growled, and gave three quick barks. The dove flew off, lighting on a ledge of rock between two torches. Kaneesh circled around and sat down below it, looking up at it.

"She's guarding us from the bird," said Demetria. "Why would she need to...?"

But Lucius had already put a grammarstone in his sling. He whirled it and threw it at the chest. "*Lapis scindens thesaurum.*" *The stone splitting the chest.*

The stone glanced off the chest and angled off to the other

side of the cavern. The dove flew up and then toward it, but Kaneesh barked and made it come back to its perch.

Another stone. "*Thesaurus apertus.*" *The chest, opened.*

Again, nothing.

Kaneesh whined. The dove purred.

"Try something else," Demetria said.

"*Baculum manibus magi magistri vento,*" *May the staff be in the hands of the master mage by the wind.*

The chest lifted, and dust flew out from under it, carried by the wind Lucius had created. But after a moment, the wind subsided and the chest fell with a thud.

Kaneesh barked again, this time at Demetria and Lucius.

"We have no way of knowing," said Lucius.

Now the dove flew again to the chest, and Kaneesh kept her silence.

Prrrr prrrrr.

"She has won," said Lucius.

"Wait," said Demetria. "Is *thesaurus* not a Greek word? That's what you've been using, isn't it? Use the Latin word."

"Of course! Logo called it a *thesaurus*, and he's Greek." Lucius slung a grammarstone. "*Arca aperta!*" *The chest, opened.*

The grammarstone disturbed the dove, making her beat her wings and hover for a moment, but the chest did not open.

Kaneesh lay down on all fours now.

"It's not an *arca*," Demetria said. "It must have a special name."

"An Etruscan name?" said Lucius.

Kaneesh barked and wagged her tail.

"If so, we cannot open it with Latin!" Demetria said. "And it would be the wisest thing an Etruscan ever did! I would be very surprised if you could make a Latin grammar with an Etruscan word. They don't mix!"

The dove walked about the top of the chest, cooing gently.

"We will try anyway!" Lucius cried, and took another grammarstone. "I am half-Etruscan, after all. *Shuntheruza aperta.*" It was the Etruscan word for "box," and the Latin for "opened."

Nothing.

"We must take it," Demetria said. "Take it from here. Maybe Logo will know--"

The dove flew up, and Kaneesh raised a storm of barking. But it didn't seem to matter. The bird lit on the chest, and settled there until Kaneesh went silent, and the echoes of the barks stopped as well.

Demetria had been thinking all this time that a bird-- so small, so delicate-- could not guard the chest, but stomething stopped her from shooing it away herself. Now she decided to do it.

As she approached, the dove cooed, softly and gently as it always had.

"I wouldn't," Lucius warned.

Just as she was about to touch the chest, the dove ruffled its feathers. And in Demetria's mind's eye, she saw something that almost made her black out with fear. She fell back, stunned.

"What is it?" Lucius cried. He went to her side. She sat with her elbows propping herself up, eyes open, but seeing nothing.

"It was..." Demetria shivered. "I saw myself... Don't go near it, Lucius. It's horrible." She shook her head but the image was still there. "It was death," she said. "She made me see death."

She crossed her legs under her feet, and Lucius took her hand.

"The bird..." Lucius began.

"It is Vanth. The goddess. Nothing..." A wave of exhaustion fell over her. She tried to get up, but couldn't.

Lucius stood up and put a grammarstone in his sling. "All is not lost. It cannot be, if Rome is to be great. If Latin cannot defeat Etruscan, then let Etruscans do it. *Gemelli milites--*" *May the twin warriors...*

Across the room, a glow came from the golden lines that made up the picture of the warriors.

"What, the twins?" Demetria cried. She tried to rise again, but her legs were jelly. "What can they do? They are her servants! Stop, Lucius! You will make them attack us!"

"*Baculum manibus magi magistro...*" *The staff in the hands of the master mage...* He was almost finished, and ready to let the grammarstone go. The last word of the grammar would perfect it. But would it do what he wished it to do?

Demetria looked down at the mirror. The Turan side was glowing. And it was the figure of Atunis.

And before Lucius spoke the last word of the grammar and slung the stone, there was a knocking at the bronze doors. They opened, and a wind came in with them.

"What?" Demetria said.

The outline of a man appeared in the doorway. The whisper of his voice came: "I seek rest."

"Marcus?" Lucius said. It was almost a whimper.

The dove fluttered from up from the box, and flew over to the spirit. The spirit held up its hand, and the dove lit on it.

Then the spirit began to walk toward them, and it looked like it was going to pass by without turning its head left or right. The dove fluttered to keep its balance on the spirit's wrist.

Then, on the other side of the cavern, the portal inside the *dokana*, opened, and glowing warriors separated themselves from the rock, as if walking out from a curtain of water.

Demetria could not believe her eyes.

The warriors left their feet, flew over the chest, and flanked the spirit as it moved toward the dokana. As it came to the threshold, it turned. "*Vale*. Farewell, my brother," it said. "Farewell, sister. *Vale*. It is finished."

"Marcus!" Lucius cried.

The bird and the spirit-- and the warriors behind them-- went through the portal, and it closed.

"Marcus," Lucius said, and fell to his knees.

Kaneesh began barking up a storm. She came over to Lucius, jumped up on him, and then ran over toward the box. She put her paw on the top of it, and barked again.

Demetria cried, "Don't you see! Marcus has done it! Vanth is no longer here! We can take the chest!" She ran to the platform and put her hand on the chest. "It's so smooth. Like an eggshell. Feel it, Lucius."

Lucius looked up. There were tears in his eyes.

"Don't you see!" Demetria held our her hand to him. "He helped you. He helped us. He helped Rome, Lucius!"

Lucius looked into Demetria's eyes.

"For Rome, Lucius!" she pleaded.

He was at her side. "And for Marcus," he said.

They transferred their hands below, slipping fingers between the shiny black and the marble.

"It is very light," said Demetria.

"We can take it with us," said Lucius.

They locked eyes, then both looked up.

"Does it go to the surface?" Lucius asked.

"We will see," said Demetria.

They picked up the chest. It was hardly heavier than the *baculum* would've been.

"*Magus magister et Graeca solem videntes vento.*" *Master mage and Greek woman seeing the sun, on the wind.*

They all began to rise, all except Kaneesh. Dust filled the room, but just as they were taken up, Kaneesh stole the mirror from Demetria's hand.

Demetria looked down. Kaneesh had the mirror in her teeth, Turan side up. And no longer was there a Turan on the mirror. It was glowing and melting to nothing.

"Look!" Demetria cried.

"Turanquil will not know where we are!" Lucius said. "Hold the chest between us. We will see how fast we fly."

Demetria clutched Lucius' neck with one hand and held on to the chest with the other. Lucius circled his arm around her back and held her by the waist. The thrill at his touch and the smell of the chest, like fresh-cut cedar, drunkened her. They rose, ever faster, up above the torchlight, into darkness. Demetria leaned into Lucius until her cheek touched his temple. Beside them, the chest seemed to glow, almost as if its dark surface was even darker than the darkness.

It was not long before a point of light appeared above them. They flew faster and faster. And in the next instant they were in dazzling sunshine, with the wind in their faces, cool but not nearly as cold as underground.

"Thank the gods!" cried Demetria into Lucius' ear.

Lucius let a grammarstone go in the place where he wanted them to land-- saying the important word *incolumes-- unharmed--* at the end of it.

The fell through a canopy of oak trees and onto wet grass, letting go the chest. They rolled and came to a stop, and both of them cried for joy.

The chest lay a few paces away, shining black, out of place in the spring landscape of green grass and wildflowers.

"You deserve a kiss," Demetria said to Lucius, and gave him one.

Lucius held her in his arms. "Why would I ever wish for your mouth to be closed?"

"Not so simple, you are," she said, and lifted her mouth to his again.

::XXIV::

Lucius Junius Brutus rejoiced in the sunlight that passed through the canopy of oaks and pines, the fresh, living scent of evergreen and leaf mulch. The darkness, Tuchulcha, Vanth, all of it seemed to have been wiped away-- all of it, except for the spirit of Marcus. He was with him, and always would be.

Lucius' eye fell on the chest, glossy black. They-- he and Demetria and the spirit of Marcus with them-- would open it and retrieve the *baculum*. Then they would retrieve the Shield. For Rome. And for Marcus.

"Where are we?" Demetria was lying in the grass beside him, twirling the stem of a wildflower.

"Near the top of a mountain," Lucius said, standing up. "Let's see." And he pointed up the slope.

"What about the chest?"

"Leave it here for a moment. There is nothing here but perhaps a mountain lion, and she will not take it!"

Demetria laughed at the idea, and they ran till they came, out of breath, to a rocky outcrop with no trees shading it. To the southwest, there were rings of hills encircling two lakes. Behind them, a cone of a mountain with a pinhole opening.

"That must be where we came out!" Demetria said.

To the far west, the afternoon sun was making a golden cake on the shining plate of the sea. To the north, a haze of smoke from cook fires told them where Rome was. It was a place perhaps as far from Rome as was the shrine, but to the south of it.

"I wonder how long it's been since I went underground," said Lucius, letting the warmth of the sun fill his heart.

"You were gone a day and a night before Turanquil sent me after you."

"I walked a long way. And the hippocamp took me as well."

"Hippocamp!"

Lucius laughed. "Yes! I will tell you another time. And what about you?"

"I entered the Land of the Dead at night. I expect it's been night and now it's the afternoon of the same day. I walked a long time as well."

"Well, we can fly to the shrine now," said Lucius. "I have a few grammarstones left. Then, to figure out how to open the chest."

"But at least we have the *baculum*, whether we can open the chest or not. And then we must find the Shield."

"With the *baculum* it will be easier."

Demetria hit her forehead with her open palm. "How could I forget to tell you! We do not need the *baculum*. I learned there is a grammar for retrieving the Shield."

"A grammar?" Lucius shook his head. "How so?"

"Nauarchus said that there is a special grammar that Numa

made, and that it is written on the inside of the shield handle. He said that the founder of Massalia, Protus, knew what that grammar was."

Nauarchus! How could a Greek know anything about the Shield? Lucius found himself jealous again of the sea captain, and spoke more spitefully than he wished. "And is Protus here to tell us? Or does the wise Nauarchus know?"

Demetria seemed not to notice his tone. "Let us go to the shrine, and make the chest safe. Then we can go to Nauarchus and ask about the Shield. He is in Ostia, the last I heard."

"And what of Gnaeus? Has he gone back to Portentia?"

"He told me he was going to, but he was captured by the king's men before he could. I met him at the palace when they took me there, but we said nothing to each other. Unless he has escaped, he is still there."

"Back to the shrine, then," said Lucius. "Perhaps we'll have word of him from Logo."

::XXV::

Gnaeus Portentius lay in the cell they had given him in the king's palace, wondering if he would ever get another good night's sleep.

"And my lambs," he thought. "By the gods, may someone have looked after them."

Someone would look after the lambs, he felt sure. But what about him? He had only himself to look after him, as far as he knew, and he had made something of a mess of it so far. He had left for Portentia just as the gates of the city were closing, thinking that no one would notice a lone traveler at sunset. But the guard had noticed. They had been put on notice, according to one of the men who stopped him.

"The king wants a word with you," that man had said.

But the king had not wanted a word with him. He had seen Demetria-- as if by chance-- and then been taken immediately to the room where he was and left there, in the dark, with a mattress of straw on the floor and a jug of water and round of stale flatbread next to it.

At first, Gnaeus thought he must wait for someone to come, to tell him why he was being held, but quickly it came to him that if anyone wanted him, it was the *haruspices*, for besides Lucius and Demetria he was the only one who knew where the shrine was, the place they wanted to destroy if they could.

Then, after less than a quarter hour of waiting, the door of his room opened, and a *haruspex* entered with a guard.

"Yes, it is he," said the *haruspex*. "Good work."

"O Etruscan master," Gnaeus said, "someone said the king needed a word with me. I know it is late, but I should be on my way, if--"

The *haruspex* said, "Lie down and rest. The king is seeing no one tonight."

"Still, I would--"

The guard leveled his spear at Gnaeus, who held up his hands. The *haruspex* left.

No one tonight, Gnaeus thought. It might have been an hour or two after sundown, and they expected him to sit quietly in this prison until they had need of him.

"And I don't think the king wants me," he said to the door.

His room was not a cell for holding people, but a small bedroom, perhaps for a slave. There was a window, very small, and shuttered from the outside. With a tool and light, he could reach up and undo the shutter catch, but the hole was not big enough to get through.

Gnaeus overturned the water jug and stepped up on it. He was high enough to reach the window frame and feel all around it. Yes-- there was a loose brick in the frame. He now had a job to do that meant no sleep that night.

Gnaeus was, among other things, the nephew of a master

bricklayer, and he knew that once one Roman brick was loose, others would come. As soon as he was able to worry the loose brick free, he had a tool with which he could make further headway. Working quickly, he chipped away at the mortar holding a second brick, and it fell. A third came soon after it, and then a fourth. His hands ached with the work, and more than once he smashed a finger underneath a hard brick or a brick itself, but in less than hour he was able to make a hole large enough to get both feet into including the hole in the window itself.

This was not made to hold a person who wanted to get out, he thought.

He was about the kick the shutter away when he heard a sound outside the door.

"Get him," was all he heard.

Gnaeus climbed into the window frame, kicked at the shutter with all his might, and was rewarded with a blast of cool air from the night breeze.

"*Salve et vale*," he said. "Hail and farewell."

He scrambled out, feet first, and fell something farther than he wanted to-- at least as much as his height, and turned his ankle. But he picked himself up and was running in a few seconds, despite the pain.

"Never will I tell where the shrine is," he said. "And never go back to that mirror world."

He looked back long enough to see light coming from the window where he'd escaped, then ran with his head down.

The back side of the king's palace ran down the south slope of the Palatine, and he began to slide when he could, through grass and mud, finally rolling end over end until he was stopped by a stone wall.

Gnaeus would've liked to cry out in pain, but he could hear guards coming after him, and he bit his lip to stop himself. He was able to stand, and peered over the wall. Roofs could be seen following the slope of the hill.

"Not that way," Gnaeus said. He took a left turn, following the stone wall, and finally turned south again when the neighborhood ended and yielded to pastures and groves. He was near the sacred grove of Egeria and the path that would take him back to Portentia, but there was a palisade there and a tower, and the palisade ran from the river to the slopes of the Caelian Hill, next to the Palatine.

He made his way through the grove, said a prayer to Egeria, and finally found himself near the banks of the Tiber River. The guards' cries could no longer be heard, and the only sound beside an occasional nightingale was the river itself, making a murmur that was unmistakable.

"Tiberinus! Help me!" He called to the sacred sound, which he believed was a god.

He scrambled through a grove of poplars, and his sandals slapped in puddles. The winter rains had made the river flood here, and Tiber was now ebbing back, as spring and the sun strengthened.

Gnaeus picked his way north, seeking a sandy place in the riverbank, looking for a certain something that would help his escape. He waded here and there, the cold water a shock to his skin, but good for soothing his turned ankle.

Soon he found his salvation-- a large piece of driftwood crowning a sandbar.

"Thank you, god!" he said, testing the log, a piece of poplar with the papery bark stripped off. He took hold of it by a knob of wood where a branch had once sprouted and grown strong, and dragged it down to the river.

The log floated well. Gnaeus pushed it out toward the current, blew hard as he let himself into the water up to his neck, and held on to the log. The river took him quickly.

Gnaeus thanked Tiberinus again, and said another prayer to any other god that might be listening to help him not to freeze to death before he found his way out of Rome. Fortunately, the Tiber was high, but because of that not too fast. Still there were tricky currents and eddies, and it was all Gnaeus could do to hold on as the river took him in circles, and forced him through flumes. He was able to hold on to that knob he'd used to pull the log, even when the other came free.

Finally, when he had put considerable distance between himself and Rome, and could stand the cold no longer, he made his way to the south side of the river, kicking toward it in the sluggish water, and finally splashed out on a bankside. He shivered violently as the evening air hit him, but he hoped there were farmsteads along the river, with good people who would not turn away a stranger.

At one of these, he was welcomed, and given hospitality without questions, as was the way of the people of Latium.

"Gods save Demetria and Lucius," he said as he lay covered in a fleece before the hearth fire, the family ranged about him, all sleeping save for one little girl, who stared at him without speaking before the god of sleep finally conquered her spirit.

He had made a promise to himself he would rise early and find a better hiding place, but he was so exhausted that the sun was very high in the sky before he woke. The father and the boys were in the fields pruning vines, and the mother and her girls were tending and milking goats in their yard.

After putting on his clothes that had dried well before the fire, he went outside, saw the high, strong sun, and knew he had to make a plan quickly.

"Which way is Ostia?" he asked the mother.

She looked at him as if he was crazy, and pointed to the river.

"Strangers usually come in a boat," she said, "not after a swim."

"I thank you, mistress," he said.

She nodded, and went back to milking.

Gnaeus weighed his options. There was no going back to Rome, or even to Portentia, as long as Turanquil and the *haruspices* were hunting him. But Demetria had said that Nauarchus, her future husband, was at Ostia refitting his ships. He did not really know Nauarchus, but if anyone was willing to give him shelter-- and hide him if need be-- until Demetria and Lucius returned, it would be him.

The easiest thing was to hail a barge going downriver, but he didn't want to risk being seen there. The fact that he had slept and soldiers had not come to the house where he stayed made him feel as if they had stopped looking, but he couldn't be sure. The *haruspices* had many ways of finding the truth, whether with soldiers helping him or not. He supposed that the only reason they had not yet found the shrine was because of the power of the grammarstones.

This is why they feared Rome so much.

"But if I wanted to walk to Ostia?" he asked the mother.

She pointed to a path toward their fields and said, "At the

end of this one, there is a cart track."

Gnaeus looked off to where she pointed, but hesitated. Any road would be dangerous.

Then the girl who had been staring at Gnaeus the night before piped up. "Mama, mama." She had a little switch that she was using to keep the goats from straying.

"Shhh, *puella*, bring me the next nanny goat."

"Mama. What about the secret road?"

"Shhh, you are a pest, little cabbage."

Gnaeus eyed the woman, and she eyed him back. The girl stood rolling the switch in the palm of her hands.

"She is dreaming," said the woman.

"And yet, if there is a secret road, I am much in need of it."

"Did you kill someone in Rome? Is that why you had to dunk yourself in the dark of night?"

"No, mistress," he said. "To the contrary. It is a long tale to tell, but if I am found, it will go ill for Rome."

"You talk like someone from the hill country," she said. "The old speech, the way my grandfather spoke. With these Etruscans on the Palatine, visitors speak more and more a tongue no god has ever heard."

He nodded, and thought he would delight her if he could weave some tale against the king and his people. But he could not let her know anything, lest anyone ask her. "I feel shame before you," he said, "for you have given me the hospitality of a god, and I would give you something in return. But I must be on my way, mother, before they catch me. Lives hang in the balance."

She gave a little snorting laugh. "By Father Tiber, I could not deny the secret road to one who calls me mother."

The woman instructed one of her girls to get Gnaeus a barley loaf and a chunk of goat cheese, and another to fetch a cup of water. "This farm is not big enough to keep such a big family," she said. "If you use the secret road, we expect you to pay the toll. But this little one likes you, I think." She motioned to the one with the switch. "She has always known the will of the gods."

She looked up at them, her dirty cheeks bright and hard with a smile.

"She will show you to the path. Look neither right nor left. You may have someone else who wants you to pay the toll."

"I will return and will pay you twice over what you ask," said Gnaeus.

"Better yet, never come back and never speak a word about this," said the mother.

The little girl ran before him down toward the riverbank, where river traffic could easily be seen, barges going upriver by hard rowing, and downriver easily, floating. The girl disappeared into a stand of reeds almost as tall as trees. When he got to the place, a muddy track had opened up, and she was on it, a little sprout among giants.

"Follow this," she said. "It is wet, but not flooded. Father Tiber goes down."

"I thank you, *puella*," said Gnaeus, and gave her a pat on the head.

"*Vale*! Farewell!" she cried, and ran like the wind back to her house.

So it was that Gnaeus Portentius took the secret road and arrived late in the afternoon, his legs caked in mud up to the knees. There were no walls around Ostia, so it was a small thing to wait till after dark and find his way into a neighborhood where a tavern keeper could find a boy to take him to the Greek quarter, on the promise of money that Gnaeus hoped Nauarchus would provide.

When they arrived in the Greek quarter, a man standing in the street was able to tell him where Nauarchus was lodging. "His second guest this day," said the man. "Have you a coin, and I will tell you more."

"No," said Gnaeus. "But when Mercury blesses me, I will find you."

"That's what everyone says about Mercury," said the man. "A pity, for it comes to a good story." He pointed.

It was a guesthouse, sturdily built, with a front door flush with the street. He knocked, and a slave answered.

"Are you Gnaeus Portentius?" the slave asked.

Gnaeus nodded.

"Stand aside," said someone behind the slave.

The slave pivoted, so that Gnaeus could see into the hearth room. The fire was glowing, and candles and lamps were lit. A figure moved into the way of the light, and for a second was only a silhouette.

"Welcome, Gnaeus," said Turanquil.

::XXVI::

Logophilus, keeper of the shrine of Numa Pompilius, was tending his vegetable patch when he caught sight of one of the stranger prodigies he'd ever seen: a pair of youths flying toward him, clutching a small box.

He had not been thinking of Demetria and Lucius at that moment. He was wondering where Kaneesh was. She had not appeared when Logo cooked breakfast that morning, and there was evidence that animals-- a deer, a rabbit-- had been able to feast that night on the newly-sprouted plants in the garden. This was always a sign that Kaneesh had gone roaming, for she was the best watchdog of vegetables in Latium.

"Thank the gods," he said aloud, standing up as the youths settled on the ground close to him. His back creaked and hips ached from stooping over in the patch, but his heart leapt to see Lucius and Demetria safe.

"Well met!" cried Lucius, setting the box down and running to Logo. Demetria came soon after.

"This is a gift of the gods!" Logo said as the youths

embraced him. A flood of relief washed over him. He had not realized how much he had missed them.

"We have the *baculum*," said Lucius, pointing at the box.

"That is well, but I am rejoicing the more that you are not visiting as spirits of the dead," said Logo.

"Is Gnaeus here?" Demetria asked as they separated. "Is he safe?"

"I know nothing about Gnaeus' whereabouts or safety," said Logo. "Nor of Kaneesh's."

Lucius nodded his head vigorously. "We much many things to tell you. Of Gnaeus and Kaneesh. And much still to do."

"Are you hungry? You have the look of the living who have seen the dead." Logo took their hands. "Eat first, and then you may tell your news."

They made their way to the *casula*, and busied themselves with making a batch of barley porridge boiled in goat's milk and well seasoned with salt. When they all had their bowls in hand and had thanked the gods, the youths began their explanation, each one taking a part in telling the story, the one picking up for the other to fill in his or her own part.

Logo smiled when he heard of Nauarchus, the handsome navigator of Massalia, but when they came to the part where the Shield was stolen, he stopped them and said, "We shall need to come back to this. For it is perhaps more important than the *baculum*."

"I told you," Demetria said, turning to Lucius and spreading her hands wide.

"They cannot destroy it, can they?" Lucius asked.

"No, thanks be to Egeria. But continue on, and we will speak of this in good time."

Finally they came to Gnaeus. "He said he was going to return to you secretly," said Demetria. "He knew the *haruspices* wanted to find the shrine, and could use him to do so. I was hoping he had escaped. But when I was summoned to the king's palace, he was there as well. And if he is still in the Etruscans' hands, perhaps he is even now on his way here, for they will lose no time in making him tell."

"Or worse, lost in the Mirror World as a punishment for not telling!" Lucius said.

"They would not banish him there when he is the only one who can tell them where the shrine is," said Logo. "He will not lead them here willingly. But at some point he must, and if they have the Shield, it will go ill for us even with the *baculum* and grammarstones."

"How is that?" Demetria asked.

"Now it is time for me to speak," said Logo. "I did not tell you about the Shield because I thought it would be safe. It always has been."

"And would have been," said Lucius. "Except for treachery against my brother."

Logo touched Lucius' shoulder. "He is a great hero for Rome, and will be remembered."

Demetria put her arm around Lucius as Logo began his story.

"Long ago, when Egeria showed Numa Pompilius the power of the Latin language and the grammarstones, he understood in his wisdom that if the stones fell into the wrong hands, they could be used for terrible ends."

"Of course, Glyph told me as much," said Lucius.

"Of course! So Numa consulted with the goddess, and

created a shield that had even more power than the grammarstones. It could not be used to perfect grammars, but it defends against them perfectly. No one who has the shield can be harmed by any grammar, and in fact, if the shield is within sight of a mage, any grammar that mage perfects will be reflected back to him and he will suffer the ill effects of it."

"Like an Etruscan mirror," said Demetria.

"Very like it!" said Logo. "But no one need have the skill to hold the mirror and deflect the stone. What's more, even grammars that attack indirectly, as you have done before, would have no effect on the bearer of the shield."

"But what about the story that it fell from the sky?" Lucius wanted to know.

"A story, nothing more! To conceal the true nature of the shield, but to help Romans understand how important it is to guard and preserve. As long as there are grammarstones, there will be a need for the Shield."

"One other thing," Demetria said. "My betrothed, who is from Massalia--"

Logo wondered again at the thought of Demetria marrying. As a Greek man, he was naturally happy for her, though he knew she was not. "Massalia! A long way away, and yet a rich place. "

Demetria humphed. "He was not my choice." She took her arm from Lucius' shoulder. "Not that he is not a fine man."

Lucius seemed to be working very hard to scrape the last porridge out of his bowl.

"Well," Demetria said, shrugging her shoulders, "Nauarchus told my family that his ancestor once was permitted to see the Shield, and was told there was a grammar on the inside of the handle that would summon the Shield to the one who spoke it."

"Yes," said Logo. "That is a defense in case it was stolen. The true owner knows the grammar, and when the shield is named correctly, it is the one grammar against which it cannot defend."

"Do you know how to name it correctly?" asked Lucius.

"I do not. Glyph never told that to me."

"Is it perhaps somewhere written on a scroll in the caverns?"

"It might be."

"We must find this grammar-- or the Shield itself," Lucius said. "Do you think the *haruspices* know its power?"

"If they do, and they bring it here," said Demetria, "then we cannot hold the shrine against them."

Logo nodded. "And we come full circle to what I said at first. We must hope that Gnaeus delays the seers, and think of something as a defense. The scrolls may help us. In the meantime, you both must rest."

"I mustn't--" Lucius began, but slumped over, and dropped his bowl.

"You see?" said Logo. "You are a master mage, but you cannot perfect grammar with a mind clouded with a spirit of fatigue."

Demetria spoke now, with urgency. "Lucius was in the Land of the Dead longer than I. Let him rest, and when he wakes, he can search for the grammar of the Shield among the scrolls. I can go to Nauarchus and be back as quickly as a bird. Lucius can perfect a grammar to let me fly to Ostia."

"I think not," said Logo, but he did not exactly know why--

perhaps he was reluctant to let his niece go away so soon into danger.

Lucius said, "Let her go; she is learning the lore as well."

Demetria again linked arms with Lucius. "See, the master mage approves it!"

Logo felt his heart and spirit stiffen. "No, this time you must listen to me. Flying to Ostia?"

"Logo, you know she will not listen to you. She listens to no one but herself!"

Demetria scowled and stamped her foot, so that everyone laughed, even Demetria in the end, and Logo knew that a god had spoken to him. "At least wait till nightfall, so that no one sees you flying. We do not need to get anyone talking about flying maidens."

"Yes, Logo," said Demetria.

After they stowed the chest in Glyph's caverns and Lucius had laid down in Glyph's old bed, Demetria took a nap in Logo's hut, and as the sun was setting had a quick meal of flatbread and dried figs.

"Hold a grammarstone in your hand at all times," said Lucius before he slept. "And the grammar will be, *Graeca domui nautae Graeci vento. The Greek woman at the house of the Greek sailor on the wind.*"

"Thank you!" Demetria said, adjusting the belt around her waist. "And Logo-- watch for Kaneesh! She has a mirror I have to return."

"I will watch," Logo assured her. "But you, be careful. And don't forget *incolumis*! If you forget that, then you will tumble down from the sky and dash your brains out."

"Yes, of course!" Demetria said. She embraced Lucius and

Logo. "I go to Nauarchus."

"Betrothed! I must meet him."

"You will," she said. "I will be back-- maybe even with the shield. And one day we will all have a feast of celebration."

"A marriage feast?"

Demetria rolled her eyes.

"Be careful, dear niece!" said Logo, embracing her again.

"Don't worry."

But Logo did worry.

::XXVII::

The cool, evening air chafed at Demetria's cheek as she flew to Ostia. The wind underneath her pushed at her feet, as if she was swimming, and while she half-stood, half-crouched on the pillar of air, she had more than enough time to think about what to do and say when she met Nauarchus again.

She hoped Nauarchus could help her find the Shield, but actually seeing him again made her head spin. These last days she had been able to put him out of her mind, but his charge to her was still there.

If you don't want me, I will go back to Massalia.

When she was with Lucius, there was no question. It was almost as if they were already married. But what of when she would see Nauarchus again? If they could defeat the *haruspices*, and there was no more need of her as partner of the great Master Mage of Rome, then perhaps it would be time to begin her life as Demetria, wife of a kind and handsome Greek captain from Massalia.

In less than an hour the wind began to ease her down, as if

opening its palm.

"I will never go on foot-- or even by horse-- again," she thought, "if I can fly. But may the gods give me luck!" And she thought of the days gone by when she was a carefree little girl, inside a thicket of bushes and playing priest and handmaid with a prince of Rome, praying to the God of Everything. "May that one go with me, too!" she said, landing on muddy ground next to a house that blazed with light despite the late hour.

As she came up to the house, she couldn't be sure that this was the right one, but she trusted the grammar, and was overjoyed to see Nauarchus answer the door.

"Is it you? Oh, my heart!" he cried as he embraced her.

Demetria hadn't expected that, though when she was in Nauarchus' arms she did not pull away. She thought of Lucius again, and that thought, in addition to the fact that Nauarchus squeezed her very tightly with strong, well-shaped arms, took her breath away.

"I can't believe it," Nauarchus kept saying. He led her into the hearth room, where he and his crew were sitting on benches with wine cups. "Is it you, or is it a demon?"

"It is I," Demetria managed, red-faced, as Nauarchus led her to the fire.

"Thank the gods. We have just been taking counsel about what to do next," Nauarchus said, and, despite the large number of thanksgivings he gave the gods, he managed to tell the story of the visit of Turanquil and the re-capture of Gnaeus.

"They showed me a picture of you in a mirror, of you walking through the darkness," said Nauarchus. "They told me you were in the Mirror World, the world of the genius."

"They lied," said Demetria, who took a wine cup and warm fleece and sat down close to the fire, suddenly aware of how cold it had been to have the wind in her face for an hour.

"I have no words," said Nauarchus, who stood beaming and shaking his head in disbelief.

"Nauarchus," said Demetria, after taking a sip of wine, "how long ago did the Etruscans leave?"

"Not long," said Nauarchus. "It was just after dark when Gnaeus came, and they left soon after that."

"How?"

"On horseback."

"Then there may be a little time."

"For what?"

"Tell me, were the Etruscans carrying any baggage? Perhaps something as big as a warrior's shield?"

"Yes, one of them was carrying something tightly wrapped, on his back."

"We were calling it a turtle shell," said one of the men.

"Yes, Tritodorus, exactly," said Nauarchus. "We didn't ask about it, but we noticed it."

Demetria sighed. "All right. Now tell me, Nauarchus, do you remember that night when you were talking about the Shield of Numa?"

"That night?"

"When you were waiting for me to come home, and you were next to the fire in our courtyard, talking about your ancestor Protus."

"You heard that?"

"Yes, yes, Nauarchus. Now I want you to think. You told my father that there was a grammar written on the inside of the shield's handle."

"Yes, but--"

"Do you remember anything about it?"

"Protus never told anyone the grammar, but--"

"But?"

When my grandfather told the story, he always called the shield *ancilia*, a word I have never heard in Latin before. He always used that word, never another one, though there are many for shield in Latin-- *clipeus*, *scutum*, and others."

"You know your Latin, Nauarchus," said Tritodorus.

"It is well, to do business with the Romans," said someone else.

Demetria shushed them. "You're sure-- *ancilia* is the word?"

"*Ancilia*, yes. Absolutely sure."

"Then I will have to try."

"Try?"

Demetria walked out of the house and to the patch of ground where she had landed. She reached into the pouch of grammarstones, and--

"What is it?"

"My grammarstones," she said. She felt around in it. She had been sure there were at least two and maybe three the last time she had used it. But now there was only one.

Then she remembered-- she had used them all with Charon, and had put one in her hand for the journey to Nauarchus' and one in the pouch for the return.

Now she had a choice-- use the grammarstone to retrieve the shield, or to return to the shrine.

If we don't get the Shield-- the ancilia, she thought, *then it won't matter whether I am at the shrine or not.*

And yet, shouldn't the shield be close by if she was to name it?

But she had the true word: *ancilia.*

And then, would it not be glorious if she, who had found the true word for the shield, could bring it back to Logo and Lucius as she had almost promised her uncle?

Demetria held the grammarstone in her hand, thought of the grammar, and spoke it: "*Ancilia manibus Graecae vento.*" *May the* ancilia *be in the hands of the Greek woman on the wind.*

"There," she said. "It may not come right away, but if I am right about the grammar, it will come."

Nauarchus stood there with the torch, his jaw dropping.

"You never said--"

"We have not told you many things. But now I suppose you are ready to sail away from this place. You do not want a wife who knows how to perfect Latin grammars."

Nauarchus shook his head. "By Zeus, I would say that I do. If you can make a shield come to you just by saying so, what else can you do?"

"I am not really the mage," said Demetria. "Lucius is. Really, I am only his handmaiden." Had she really said handmaiden? She had.

"Demetria, I knew you were an extraordinary girl," said Nauarchus. "And Aphrodite has given me a desire for you. We will be married, and together we can make Massalia and Rome the greatest nation that has ever been. The Etruscans think they have a great fleet of ships, but wait until we summon faster and better. We will never have to pay duties to them again. They will pay duties to us."

Demetria did not really take in what Nauarchus said-- she

was concentrating on the grammar, anxious for it to work. If she had, she would have seen a man completely at her feet. She tapped her foot, then said, "Nauarchus, *ancilia*. That was the name of the shield?"

"Of course. Did you not--"

"Well, in case my grammar was not perfect, do you happen to have a horse?"

"Yes-- and they are saddled. We were going to follow Turanquil and her people, though they threatened to hurt you if we did."

"Threatened?"

"We can go with you, as many as you wish," said Nauarchus. "I am going, certainly."

"But I must go alone."

"I will not lose you again, love," said Nauarchus. "Even if you will not listen when I tell you you are extraordinary."

Demetria rolled her eyes, but inside it was her stomach that was jumping up and down. Extraordinary? She must learn to listen to Nauarchus more closely.

"All right, then," said Demetria. "Let us fly."

::XXVIII::

It took a long time for Lucius to yield to the spirit of sleep.

After all that he'd been through underground, and the challenges still ahead, it felt strange to be lying down in his old bed in the cavern of the shrine. Still, he knew that he would have to get some rest somehow, if he wanted to be any good in defending the shrine or finding the grammar for the Shield of Numa.

At first, he ran through all the things in his head of what had just happened, and for a while he slept, but his spirit kept seeming to return to the Land of the Dead, and he would wake with a start to realize he was not.

Then, finally, exhausted, he slept hard for several hours, but awoke with an idea in his mind that he had to try.

It was still dark, and the pre-dawn chill bit, but Lucius hardly noticed it. He carried the chest out of the cavern, past the waterfall, up the stairs, and to the quarry where he knew the power of the grammarstones would be the greatest.

"*O fulmen scindens arcam!*"

A bolt lit up the sky, followed by a boom of thunder that

seemed to roll endlessly.

But all it did was rouse Logo.

"What did I tell you about lightning bolts? You could have killed yourself," he cried when he reached the quarry.

"I do not know how to open this. I had to try."

"Did you not try in the Etruscan Land of the Dead?"

"Yes," said Lucius. "But nothing in Latin ever worked on it. At first we called it *thesaurus*, because you had."

"Yes, that is a bad habit of mine, to use a Greek word for a Latin."

"Then we called it *arca*. But it still didn't open."

Logo balled his fist. "And so that means--"

"It must have an Etruscan name. There is no other thing like it in the world. It is not an *arca*. It is its own thing."

"And Latin grammar does not work in Etruscan."

"Yes, that must be it."

"But the lightning bolt?"

"Just an idea..." Lucius rubbed his face. He was still so tired. "An idea that didn't work."

"It is a good idea. Lightning is from the gods and this chest is also. If anything could destroy the chest, it would be lightning. But you must find a way to direct the lightning to it. And *arcam* is not the proper striker this time."

Lucius blinked and squared his shoulders, proud that Logo had not scolded him this time for experimenting with the fire of Jupiter. "You speak truly. We must find an Etruscan who knows about the chest-- and convince him to give us the name."

Neither of them said anything, and the sudden, birdless quiet of almost-dawn washed over Lucius. Awed, he thanked the gods, picked up the chest, and turned with Logo toward the path down the quarry hill.

Finally, Lucius said, "It has been many hours since Demetria left, and she has not returned. With the grammarstone to help her, I think she should be back by now. I should go after her."

"You were to look for the summoning grammar for the Shield."

"Oh, yes," said Lucius. He scratched the back of his head. The prospect of spending hours in the scroll room studying appealed to him not in the least. "I will go and come back quickly," he said.

"You had better," said Logo. "We do not know where the *haruspices* are."

"Probably still in Rome," said Lucius. "Glyph always used to say, they never strike first."

"Many things have changed since Glyph spoke those words to you."

"I will be back quickly," Lucius said. "I promise."

Logo consented. It did not take the inspiration of a god to tell he wanted to know where she was, too.

He was up in the air swiftly, with a grammarstone in his hand and on his lips a grammar to bring him to the Greek girl, about whom he had made so many grammars in the past.

The sun was still not above the mountains when he could feel the grammar pulling him groundward.

He alit next to a horse with two riders, one male, astride the horse, the other one riding in front of him, side saddle.

He had his arm around her waist.

That arm made Lucius impatient, and he had hardly

acknowledged Demetria's greeting when he burst out, "Why didn't you fly back to the shrine? And what is he doing with you?"

"He," said Demetria, "is Nauarchus. If you have never met one another."

Nauarchus helped Demetria down from the horse, then got down himself.

Nauarchus seemed to Lucius very tall after only seeing him from far off.

"I have news," she said. "Nauarchus knows the name of the shield of Numa. It isn't *scutum* or *clipeus*. It's *ancilia*."

"Nauarchus knows?" Lucius said.

"Yes, my ancestor Protus told my grandfathers, and they have remembered it since," said Nauarchus.

"*Anclilia*? It is an easy word to misremember."

Nauarchus bristled. "And yet, they did not."

"*Ancilia*, not *an*-clil-*ia*," said Demetria. "It is easy to remember. I tried a grammar to make it come, but it didn't. That's why we were riding. I didn't have a grammarstone to fly back with."

Lucius was still jealous of Nauarchus, but now he was more curious. "What was the grammar you tried to perfect?"

She told him.

"There's nothing wrong with that... unless..."

"Unless what?"

"You thought *ancilia* was of the first kind-- the one with mostly letter A's in its endings and female words." And he thought of the list of possibilities in that case:

Summoner o ancilia

Namer	ancilia
Striker	anciliam
Bestower	anciliae
Builder	anciliad
Owner	anciliais
Placer	anciliai

"But it could be another kind-- the third," Lucius continued.

"How?"

There are many neithers in the third kind that end in the letters i and a. *Maria*, *seas*, is one. Another is *animalia*, animals; third *calcaria*, chalkstones. There's only one thing about them. They are all more than one." And there, in his mind's eye, was the list of those possibilities:

Summoner o ancilia	
Namer	ancilia
Striker	ancilia
Bestower	ancilibus
Builder	ancilibos
Owner	ancilium
Placer	anciliebos

"So *ancilia*-- you're saying that word means *many shields*? And that would be the word to use for the parade of twelve shields, when the priests dance with them."

"Yes. And one shield would have to be one of three things-- *ancile*, *ancilar*, or *ancil*."

"He is a master of Latin!" Nauarchus said, genuine

admiration in his voice. "But how will this make a difference?"

"It will make all the difference," Lucius said. "If you do not name something correctly, the grammar will not be perfected, and what you want will not be so."

"Then perhaps you should make this grammar now, to summon the *ancilia*."

"Or the *ancil*. Or whatever it is," said Lucius. "This must be what was meant by a secret grammar. But I think we must catch up with the *haruspices* first-- make sure Gnaeus is safe, and cast a grammarstone at the Shield to go with the grammar."

Demetria agreed it was the best plan.

Nauarchus said, "We are not far behind them, I think. When you left, they were not yet at the shrine?"

"No, there was no sign of them at all," Lucius said.

"Gnaeus can't have taken them by the most direct route," Demetria said. "I am sure he would take them on a merry chase and only bring them close when threatened."

Lucius was quick to offer the next step: "So you and I, Demetria, must go now to defeat the *haruspices*."

"Nauarchus will go, too," Demetria said.

"He is not needed."

"We will need every friend we can get."

"Friend?" said Lucius, as if he had never heard the word.

Nauarchus said, "You are a great mage to be able to fly exactly where we were. If I am not pleasing in some way to you, then perhaps you should make me fly into the sea and drown! Otherwise, I am going with you. I would be off the ground and in the air with you, but if not, I can go by horse and meet you there."

"No," said Demetria. "Don't speak about drowning or anything horrid like it. You will go with us, and this poor horse will no longer have to carry two.

Lucius said, "I have never done a grammar where three flew at the same time."

"We will all hold a grammarstone. You have three, do you not?"

Of course," said Lucius, his hand straying to the pouch at his side. For the first time ever, he wished it wasn't so full. "But you know it will be dangerous."

Nauarchus said, "I have been in gales where Poseidon's hand lifted me off the deck of my ship as I held the rudder. Danger does not cow me, especially if my love-- my friend-- needs me."

Lucius sighed. "This is not danger as you have known it. It is much worse than being on a ship."

"What do you know about being on a ship, little man?" Nauarchus said.

"I have been underwater and yet breathed! Can you do that?"

"I should be able if I have a little stone in my hand!"

Demetria stamped her foot. "Stop it! Two more stupid children have I never heard speak nonsense in my life! This is useless. You can fight if you want, but I am going to the shrine."

Lucius screwed up his mouth. Nauarchus cleared his throat. "Well?"

"Here is a grammarstone," Lucius said, reaching into his pouch. "Take it. She's right, we need to find Gnaeus. He is a friend."

"Humph," Demetria said, and stuck out her lip.

"Thank you," said Nauarchus. He took the grammarstone, closed his fist around it, and gasped. "It is alive! A wonder."

Lucius nodded and threw a glance Demetria's way. She put out her hand, and he gave her a grammarstone, too.

"You are impossible, Lucius Junius Brutus. And I am beginning to think you are, too, Nauarchus of Massalia."

"*Magus magister et Graeci loco Numae ventod incolumes*," Lucius said after they had linked arms, Demetria in the middle. *The master mage and the Greeks at the shrine on the wind unharmed.*

As they rose, Nauarchus let out a whoop. The torch of Artemidorus tightened into a point of light, then disappeared behind the summit of a hill.

"Finally!" said Demetria, closing her eyes to the wind, and tightening her grip around the arms of her men.

::XXIX::

Gnaeus' tired legs took ill the hard ride to Rome. The *haruspices* kept their horses in a trot at all times, and a canter when Turanquil ordered it. When darkness fell, they lit a torch, and a *haruspex* rode in front and in back of Gnaeus. In this way, they arrived in Rome in less than two hours, refreshed themselves with food and drink, switched horses, and were on their way toward Portentia and the shrine an hour after that.

They said nearly nothing the entire time, though Gnaeus would ask a question now and then, if only to break the silence.

"Do you think these horses can keep up this pace?"

"I am a bit thirsty."

The seers never answered with more than a couple of words, until, in the dead hour past midnight when they were finally close to their destination, Turanquil spoke, breath coming in clouds in the pre-dawn cold.

"It will soon be yours to lead the way, master Gnaeus," she said. "Even we cannot spot the turning to Portentia every time, and certainly not in darkness. The shrine, even less so."

Gnaeus had thought about this since leaving Ostia. If he had a say in it, the *haruspices* would never reach the shrine. But he need not make them believe that they wouldn't. There were many paths in the hills. And especially in the dark, they would have no idea where he was taking them.

"I will lead you there if it is truly because you are going to rescue Demetria," he said. "Otherwise..."

"Otherwise you will join her," said one of the *haruspices*.

"You shall see Demetria," said Turanquil, but she swore by no god or goddess.

Once they truly came to the hill country, the footing was too treacherous for horses, so they tied them to trees and advanced on foot.

The next few hours were spent in walking, with brief rests punctuated by scoldings and threats from the *haruspices*. At a certain point, Gnaeus confessed he was lost, and asked to stop and rest till first light. He was only half-lying about being lost. He could've found the shrine in the dark and blindfolded, but the hard travel had dulled his senses. He knew they were close, but his sluggish mind did not know how close.

Soon after that, there was a flash and a clap of thunder, perhaps two miles away.

"Lightning of Vegoia!" said Velthur, using the name of the Etruscan goddess of lightning.

"And from a clear sky," said Repsuna.

"Still your idle tongues," said Turanquil. "It comes from there--" she pointed-- "and is not far. I would swear an oath by any god that the shrine is in that place."

"It was only a prodigy," Gnaeus tried, his heart sinking. "That comes anywhere in this area, even over the town itself."

"Still, we will go that direction," said Turanquil. "And mirrors at the ready.

This was a disaster. Turanquil was right. The lightning came from just over what Gnaeus knew was the quarry. They were closer than he wanted to be, on the path toward the stump of the fig tree that marked the turnoff to the shrine.

In a half-hour, with Turanquil leading the way, they had made it to the fig.

Gnaeus had very little left he could do. But he tried.

"I cannot..." he began, stumbled, and fell to the ground.

"Call a halt," said Turanquil. "Weariness overtakes this one."

"There were no stones in his path," said Velthur.

"Will you hold your tongue?"

"But mistress--"

Turanquil balled her fist around her mirror, the tendons in her wrist tensing. The *haruspices* said no more, and they all found tree trunks to lean against. Just above the hill, there was a gray line that was the beginning of dawn.

Gnaeus knew his last chance was simply to break their will, make them give up looking. They weren't used to staying up the entire night, riding thirty miles on horseback, then walking. He knew they were desperate, that they were racing against time somehow. Stop to rest long enough, and they would all yield to their fatigue.

"Let them taste what it means to rest," he thought, "And then! If only master Lucius shows up, and Demetria with him, I hope! That lightning must mean he is back. He'll take care of these scoundrels."

And almost as if his thoughts had been heard, there was a

tiny rustle in the bushes nearby, not even big enough to be a quail. If Turanquil and the others had been less tired, they may have turned their mirrors immediately.

As it was, Gnaeus dropped to the ground. The sound of a Latin grammar came from the same place-- he couldn't hear the whole thing, just something about *haruspices*. And a grammarstone came whistling, cast from a sling.

Just as quickly, a mirror came up. Gnaeus put his arms over his head and closed his eyes tightly. He waited for the ping as the stone hit the mirror, but it didn't.

The stone flew over, making a buzzing sound, then crackled as it came flying back to where it had been thrown.

From there, when the grammarstone hit with a little thud, came a cry of pain, an *arrrghh!*, and the *haruspices* cried out in triumph.

They ran down to the bush. Gnaeus was close behind.

There was Logo, bound on all sides with ropes, as tight as you like.

"It is the poet!" Velthur cried. "The assistant of the teacher, Glyph."

"Logophilus," said Logo, grunting with the tightness of the bonds.

"But no one deflected that Roman rock," said Repsuna. "Did you get your mirror on it?"

"No indeed," said Velthur.

Turanquil said, "Nor did I. It bent back of its own accord. We are in a land of wonders. It will all be explained to us when we get to the shrine. Finally, the gods of Etruria triumph."

"Master!" Gnaeus said. "Was that your grammar?"

Logo nodded, and scowled. "And it was a good one. It

should have worked, if not for--" but he didn't finish his sentence. "Still, I had to try."

Turanquil looked down at Logo, then at the muddy track he had left behind him. "To the shrine," she said. "You were right, Gnaeus. It was not far."

::XXX::

"I can see the sun rising!" Nauarchus yelled over the wind. "It is a wonder! A god's doing!"

"And I can see smoke rising," said Lucius, who was looking down. The blur of tears that the wind had created still allowed him to see the clearing and Logo's vegetable patch as they neared it, and it was clear someone had set a fire.

Demetria said, "Perhaps it is Logo's cooking fire."

"It looks too thick and black for that," said Lucius.

As they alit near the *casula*, they realized the fire was made of bookcases-- and scrolls-- and a *haruspex* whose bare, bald held identified him as Velthur, was tending it with a long stick. The blaze was bright, and the flames licked up high; the pile of ash was already a dark stain on the ground. Another *haruspex*-- Repsuna-- was coming from the caves with an armload of scrolls.

"The knowledge of Numa!" Lucius screamed. He ran toward the fire, got out his sling, and cast a grammarstone into it. "*O aqua extinguens ignem!*" *I summon water putting out the fire.*

A bubble of water-- as big as a cow or horse-- appeared above the flame, fell on it with a whoosh. A thick cloud of white smoke rose from the fire, and Velthur was engulfed in it.

Repsuna dropped the scrolls and ran, but Lucius said *o radices pedem haruspicis tenentes*," I summon roots to hold the feet of the *haruspex*, and tree roots shot up and twined themselves around Repsuna's ankles. He went headlong, falling on his face.

Velthur crawled out from the cloud of smoke, coughing.

"If you've harmed Logo," Lucius said, poising a grammarstone at him.

"Over here," came a cry. It was Gnaeus. He was in the *casula*, tied tight. Nauarchus knelt next to him, took out a knife, and began cutting at the bonds.

"I can do that faster," said Lucius.

"No," said Demetria, laying her hand on his arm. "Turanquil. She must have taken Logo. You will need your grammarstones for her."

Nauarchus cut the last rope that bound Gnaeus' hands behind him. He groaned, and flexed his arms. "She is in the quarry. These were Logo's bonds, but they untied him and made him go with them down to the caverns. They have the Shield, master."

"How do you know? Did you see it?" Demetria asked.

"Yes, one of the seers was carrying it."

"You'll soon be free," said Nauarchus, now working on the knots around Gnaeus' feet and ankles.

"I thank you, good sir," said Gnaeus. "Who are you?"

Nauarchus laughed. "Go, youths. I will finish this job.

Lucius and Demetria jumped up.

"And one other thing," Gnaeus said. "They took the grammarstones master Logo just made."

"What does she think she can do with them?"

"She didn't say. But before they went, she kept saying how the place was filled with power."

Lucius and Demetria ran up the stone stairs from the caverns to the quarry. It was a disaster that some scrolls were lost, but it would be much worse if Turanquil managed to destroy the staff or the shield or both.

The rising sun was tingeing the quarry cliffs soft pink and orange, and as they crested the hill and looked down into the opening between the cliffs, they caught sight of Turanquil standing over the chest, which was still closed. The Shield was propped on the lid of the chest, its metal accoutrements glinting dully. Logo was standing next to her, looking as miserable as ever he had.

"Stop!" Lucius cried. He loaded a grammarstone into his sling, his mind casting around for a grammar that matched his anger.

Turanquil raised her mirror. "Stay your hand, Roman," she said. "Think of your treasures." And she used her free hand to point out the staff and the shield.

"Roman!" Demetria cried. "And you told me before you wanted to save him because he was Etruscan!"

"Come, Logo," Lucius said.

Logo glanced at Turanquil, but she held up her mirror. "Go," she said. "You will be back with me in no time. The mirror will bend your feet."

Logo hung his head.

"Stay your tongue, Lucius Junius," Turanquil said. "You

know this place has power-- more than any other place because of the grammarstones, which I now have."

Gnaeus and Nauarchus joined the youths on the crest of the hill.

"Do you not think that this mirror can bring fire from the sky?" Turanquil was saying. "And with the grammarstones aiding--"

"But the shield reflects--" Lucius began.

Gnaeus put his hand up, and whispered "Kaneesh!" to Lucius.

The dog was scrambling down a path in the rocks, Demetria's mirror still in her teeth.

Turanquil had not seen Kaneesh yet. "I see you were not able to open the *shapatanasar.* That is its name. It cannot be opened by Latin grammar. But I can open it, and I can destroy your staff. Lightning is of the gods, and that is the only thing that can destroy what is of the gods."

"What do you want us to do?" Demetria said.

"This one will help me take the shield and staff back to Vanth," Turanquil said, pointing to Logo. "If you value his life, you will do nothing to stop me. Rome will be for the Etruscans-- and Etruria will be ours, with our gods supporting it. Then you must leave this shrine forever, leave the scrolls and the grammarstones, and never do another grammar again. We would not kill the last son of the Junius clan, a scion of royal Etruscan blood. But you must renounce your Roman nature, and join with us to be the true rulers of Rome."

Lucius' fury boiled. "Join you-- when you killed my brother?"

"He attacked us," Turanquil said. "Are you saying we

cannot defend ourselves? He became an enemy, but Lucius, we do not have to be enemies. You can be king."

"What about Arruns? He is the prince now. Are you going to kill him, too?"

"He is weak and ill. He will not live long, even if he does become king. You are the next-- and last-- Tarquin after him."

Logo said, "Turanquil. I do not know how to get to the Etruscan Land of the Dead from here."

"But they do. And they will show me, for your sake and the sake of this." Again she pointed at the *shapatanasar* and the Shield. "It is all one to me whether the shield and the staff are the property of Vanth or destroyed. Either way, Rome is for Etruria. Think on that."

Kaneesh had stopped some fifty paces behind Turanquil, dropped the mirror, and sat down, blinking.

Demetria leaned to Lucius' ear, her hand shielding her mouth. "Summon the shield. She'll have nothing defending her then. And the *baculum* is still safe inside the chest."

"If I bring up my sling, she'll call down lightning and destroy herself and Logo," Lucius said. "Besides, we don't know which is the right ending for the shield. Is it *ancile*, *ancilar*, or *ancil*?"

Kaneesh howled. Turanquil, startled, turned.

And a grammar came from Lucius' mouth.

"*Ancile manibus magistri magi ventod!*"

The shield in the hands of the master mage on the wind.

The grammarstone flew from the sling directly at the back of Turanquil's head. When it reached her, it dissolved into a sphere of golden light. It only lasted for a moment, just longer than a flash of lightning might, and when it winked out, the shield stood up on its own and flew like a discus toward Lucius.

Logo yelped, and dived out of the way as fast as his spindly limbs could take him.

Turanquil turned, screamed, and pointed her mirror at the sky. "Vegoia, the fire of the gods!" she cried.

Lightning flashed from the clear sky and crackled toward the shield just as it flew onto Lucius' outstretched arm, like a falcon returning to the hand of its master.

The lightning arrived almost at the same moment. The impact of it shook Lucius and made his head buzz madly, but he was able to stand.

There was a boom, and then another, as the lightning arced back toward Turanquil.

Finally, another flash, and an explosion that bowled everyone over. A wave of shards struck them, something like pottery and wood and metal at the same time, along with thick, sour smoke.

Lucius lay there with his hands over his ears, his knees tight up against his chest, his neck stinging where something sharp had cut him. His ears rang. He coughed through the smoke, and waited for the breeze to catch it up and fetch it away. The only sound was a kind of popping and fizzing, and the smell of the lightning bolt, that portended rain.

Logo was the first to stand up. "Gods," he whispered.

The smoke had not quite cleared, and more was coming from where Turanquil had stood. There no longer Turanquil or the chest. Instead, there was Kaneesh, sniffing over the blackened body of the seer. Next to her, in stark contrast to the burn marks of the explosion, the silvery shaft of the *baculum*.

Gnaeus popped his head up from an outcrop of rocks. "She did it to herself!" he cried.

"To herself!" came the echo from the quarry.

Lucius looked about him, and found that Nauarchus and Demetria had fallen together, and that he had cradled her around him. Demetria stood up, red-faced, and brushed herself off. Nauarchus did the same.

"How do you fare?" Lucius said, and his voice sounded thin and weak.

"Well," said Nauarchus, the turning to Demetria, "And you, love?"

"Well," said Demetria. "Thank you... husband."

All three stared at each other without saying anything, until Logo, who didn't seem to understand the significance of what Demetria had just said, chimed in:

"That's it for Turanquil... and the chest, by Zeus."

"By Zeus indeed," said Nauarchus. "And that is it for me."

"What do you mean?" asked Demetria, suddenly alarmed.

"I mean," said Nauarchus, and wiped grimy sweat from his forehead, "that I can never again sing the songs of Homer."

"Why not?"

"Because the story of Lucius and Demetria is a greater one by far. They will sing of you in Massalia forever."

Demetria laughed, and the sun seemed to brighten, and a fresh breeze to lap at their torn cloaks. "Nauarchus. You are a great joker, I think."

Lucius had never heard her speak so affectionately to anyone before. Maybe when they were in the cavern with the bronze mirror warrior. But that seemed so long ago.

Logo said, "Lucius, you must take your prize. The *baculum*. Master Mage of Rome, fully armed and armored."

Lucius walked down the hill, and Kaneesh met him halfway. "You did well, Egeria," he said, and ran his hand over her soft ears.

Kaneesh barked, and went on toward Logo.

Lucius knelt at Turanquil's body and said a prayer to his ancestors, the Lares. Turanquil's spirit would be flying down to Charon now, and she would meet Vanth soon, the bird that carries the dead to their rest.

"Welcome her," he prayed.

When he picked up the *baculum*, he felt the familiar vibration, the living power that coursed up his arm and tickled at the base of his ear. And now it was even greater, for the *ancile*, the Shield of Numa, fit snugly around his other arm.

"You are a hero," Nauarchus called down to him. "May the gods prosper you. And may Athena fly with you."

"Thank you," Lucius called back, and raised his weapons.

Logo and Gnaeus took up the job of caring for Turanquil's body, and the other three went back down the stone stairs to wash and tend to their wounds. Fortunately, the shards from the exploding chest had not cut any of them deeply.

Later, over a fire and a meal, in which Repsuna and Velthur also partook, though they remained tied up, Demetria asked the question that must have been on her mind from the moment he perfected the most important grammar of his life:

"Why did you choose *ancile* for naming the shield?"

"It is a curious thing," he said. "I turned it over and over in my mind as Turanquil spoke. I never thought of being king as she said I might be. I knew she was lying-- prettier words have never been spoken-- and the prettier they are, the worse they are."

"It is something the Greeks know well," said Logo, and Nauarchus nodded.

"I knew we would only have one chance for a grammar before she made us do her will. And so I just kept thinking back to long ago... when my father took me to the shores of our sea-- *mare nostrum*-- and how many seas is *maria*. I trusted in the genius of my father."

"Well done," said Nauarchus.

"And I have one question as well, Master Lucius," Gnaeus said. "Once we've seen the body of the *haruspica* safely back to her people and laid her in her tomb..."

"Yes?"

"May I go back to my lambs? There's no one in town can give them better care."

Logo laughed. "You may go back now, faithful Gnaeus, as far as I am concerned. You've earned a rest."

"Thanks to you, master Logo, and I appreciate your kindness," said Gnaeus, "but I think my genius wouldn't abide not to carry that lady back to Rome. You've got to give the dead their respect."

"And now, I speak," said Nauarchus, and took Demetria's hand.

Demetria caught her breath.

"I have seen such great wonders in the past day," he said. "I hardly know what to think. Flying through the air like Hermes! The language of power, making the earth and the sky do your will. And I am just a humble sailor, alive at the whim of Poseidon."

"Don't say that, husband," Demetria said. "Your skill at piloting ships--"

"--Not to be spoken of next to you and your hero. Demetria, you must stop calling me husband."

Demetria gasped. "And whyever is that?"

"Because I am not going to marry you."

"What?" Demetria drew back, her eyes wide. "It is you who gave me the choice! Do you not remember? I must decide!"

Nauarchus raised a finger. "A moment. I know I said all that. But now I have seen the reason why you did not want to marry me in the first place. And I am grateful that you would consent to have me now. But it is clear--"

Demetria balled her fist. "I can't believe this. Just when I--"

"-- that you and Lucius are a pair that should not-- cannot-- be separated. He is not of age for marrying yet, but whatever happens between you, you cannot live apart from him. The gods have put you together."

"But we've finished our quest! Rome is safe. There is nothing else to do."

Logo said, "That is not quite true."

"Oh?" Lucius said.

"This is now the moment Glyph had feared. Lucius, you are Master Mage. You can do anything. With the shield and the staff, you can be king. The question is, do you want this power?"

"We have spoken before of having no more kings," said Lucius.

"Yes, we have," said Logo. "But are you ready to give up your power-- forever?"

Lucius looked over at the artifacts he had won, which were

propped against the wall of the *casula*. The feeling of them on his arms still remained.

"Are there no more threats to Rome from the other world?"

"Few," said Logo.

"It would seem a small thing," said Lucius, but he nearly choked on the words.

"Not so small."

"The task of making Rome a place no longer of kings, but of the people," said Nauarchus. "No more tyrants? A very large task."

"Especially since Tarquin still rules," said Logo.

"I can sweep him away," said Lucius. "Bring together a group of men-- like we had at the boy's council-- to vote, to make laws, to rule the city together.

"But you must put away your power. If not, you would become a tyrant yourself."

Lucius took a deep breath, and as he exhaled he looked out at the horizon, and the trees that hid the view all the way to the city.

"Demetria can help you," said Nauarchus.

Demetria was about to speak, but instead she threw her arms around Nauarchus' neck.

Lucius was ready to hear her protests that she would do anything if only she could go with Nauarchus to Massalia.

But she didn't.

"Thank you," was all she said.

::XXXI::

"So, shall we bring the *ancile* back to Rome?" asked Demetria, after she had had her fill of embracing Nauarchus.

"Yes," said Lucius, "as long as we know where it is kept, and I can retrieve it in a time of danger."

"Best that you not retrieve it," said Logo. "And the *baculum* should be kept in a safe place as well."

"And the first one, the one full of gold! Master, I hope you hid it well," said Gnaeus.

"I did," said Lucius. "And I think it might be best for me, so as not to arouse suspicion of my powers, that I take that first one and remain a simpleton for all but my closest allies."

"This is wise," said Logo. "Tarquin is still king, and his son is still prince. They want to keep power. If they know about the staff and the shield, they may plot to kill you."

"And I?" said Nauarchus. "By Zeus, my ship will be ready to sail in a few days, and I still have to explain to both my father and yours--" he motioned to Demetria-- "that I am not going to marry after all."

Demetria said nothing, but she got a faraway look in her

eyes that Lucius knew meant she was plotting to make some trouble.

And so it was that the *ancile*, the shield of Numa, was returned by night, secretly, to the doorstep of the temple of Vesta, where the priestesses cared for the eternal flame of the Roman city. The *baculum* was kept at the shrine, where Logo might use it against prodigies. And Lucius uncovered the hiding place of the gold-filled staff: in the thicket of bushes which had been Demetria and Lucius' childhood meeting place.

"Why did you not tell me it was there?" Demetria said later.

"It wouldn't have been a hiding place then," said Lucius.

The night before Nauarchus sailed for Massalia, there was a dinner, and Demetria invited both Gnaeus and Lucius. At the end of it, Nauarchus made his announcement, that he would not marry Demetria.

"She should become a priestess at the proper time," said Nauarchus. "She is not destined to wait for a sailor to come home from the sea."

Istocles threw up his hands. "Demetria is impossible!"

"Father," said Demetria, "do you agree that Nauarchus would make the best son-in-law you could ever imagine?"

"Yes, by all the gods," said Istocles.

"Then why not marry Phane to him?" said Demetria.

Everyone gasped.

"I cannot," said Phane. "I vowed on Aphrodite that I would never marry again!"

"But Phane, you spent so much time telling me he would be a fine husband! Could he not also be a fine husband to you?"

"By Hera," said Eodice. "Phane has made her vow. We all know she has promised not to marry again. Only the gods can take it from her."

"Only the gods!" Nauarchus said. "I am willing, because of what Demetria has told me about Phane, that she is shining among women, as loyal as Penelope, who waited for Odysseus for twenty years. But I do not see the gods looking down upon us to settle this small matter."

"Nor do I," said Phane, who looked miserable.

"Phane would be a good match for this young man," said Istocles. "She is as you say, a woman as good or better than my wife."

"Husband!" said Eodice.

"By Zeus, it is true," said Istocles.

Until then, Lucius had been silent, playing his role. But he forgot himself for a moment.

"Wait a minute!" said Lucius. "What an idiot I've been. I forgot!"

"What?" Everyone said at once.

"I mean..." Lucius looked around at everyone. "Gods. Spirit. Of Aristoxenus. Message!"

"You have a message from the gods?" Istocles said.

"He sounded like he was speaking in his right mind just then," said Eodice.

"I don't think so," said Demetria.

"Nor I," said Nauarchus.

"But I--"

"Shhh, auntie. Lucius, tell us! What was the message from the spirit of Aristoxenus?"

"Eis archonta nauos gemasthai exestin."

He speaks in Greek!" said all the Greeks one after the other.

"It is of the gods," said Demetria. "A simpleton of Rome does not speak Greek."

"By Hermes, you are right this time, daughter!" said Istocles.

"What was it again?"

Lucius repeated himself.

"It means *It is permitted to marry the captain of the ship.*" said Demetria to Gnaeus, when he asked what it meant in Latin. "Aristoxenus is giving Phane permission to marry again, from beyond the grave!"

But he cannot have that quite right, said Istocles. "The master of a ship is not an *archon nauos*, but a *naukrator*."

"And I am not a captain, but only a helmsman," said Nauarchus.

"*Archonta nauos*," said Eodice. "*Nauarchus.*"

Everyone gasped again.

Demetria clapped her hands. "Of course. He wasn't saying captain of a ship-- he was saying Nauarchus."

Nauarchus laughed. "It is true! My parents wanted to call me something a little grander than simply captain. *Archon* means a chief, a commander, and a captain.

Phane's eyes shone. "I can't believe my ears!" she cried.

"Believe!" said Lucius. "Gods good."

"At least he has not completely lost his senses," said Istocles, narrowing his eyes at the one everyone now called Brutus.

::XXXII::

The sun rose from the mountains bright and shining on the June day that Nauarchus' fleet returned from Massalia. A barge took him, adorned with summer flowers, up river with strong men rowing, crowns of laurel leaves on their brows.

Nauarchus himself was clad in a chiton of finest linen, his strong legs bare, and his crown was of oak leaves, the tree of Hera, mistress of marriage.

Phane herself wore a gown woven by her sister Eodice, intended for Demetria, but altered in the time between the betrothal of Phane and Nauarchus and their wedding day.

Istocles joined them that afternoon, after Nauarchus vowed that the two Greek families of Massalia and Rome would be linked forever, and that as a sign of that link, Demetria was invited to visit Phane and him in Massalia whenever she wished.

"Perhaps we could fly there!" Demetria said later to Lucius, during the revelry that followed.

"As long as we are together," said Lucius. "I will go

anywhere with you."

Demetria laughed and caught Nausimache up in her arms. "Little one! You have found a father today!" she cried.

Nausimache, who had pulled the crown of flowers from her hair and was waving it about her in Demetria's arms, said, "Thanks be to the God of Everything!"

Lucius stared at Demetria.

"One has to teach the children about divine things," she said.

And Lucius laughed.

FINIS

ACKNOWLEDGMENTS

- Glossary of terms
- Map
- List of characters
  to reference

AUTHOR'S NOTE

45059127R00155

Made in the USA
Charleston, SC
09 August 2015

Proof